Was Lillie dreaming or was she living her nightmare?

Jason's face was barely illuminated by the faint glow of the street lights. Lillie saw anguish fill his eyes. Suddenly she felt the carriage move, and she knew that they were going over the edge.

"I love you, Lillie," were the last words Jason spoke.

"Jason!" Lillie screamed. Then amidst the noise of screaming horses and splintering wood, Lillie's head hit something hard and she lost consciousness

Lillie was lost in her nightmare again. She felt the bone-chilling cold and knew the darkness would never turn to light. She thought several times that someone was calling to her. Other times she heard crying. Where was she and why couldn't she make herself wake up? Lillie felt frightened for the first time in her life.

JANELLE JAMISON is the pen name of Tracie J. Peterson, a freelance writer and regular columnist for a Christian newspaper.

Books by Janelle Jamison

HEARTSONG PRESENTS

HP-19—A Place to Belong

Perfect Love

Janelle Jamison

Heartsong Presents

With love and thanks to my husband, Jim, for the invaluable research he did; and to my children Jennifer, Julie, and Erik for their love and support.

ISBN 1-55748-412-0

PERFECT LOVE

one

Lillie Philips placed a final hairpin in her honey blond hair and sat back to study her work. Yes, it would be perfect. Lillie felt a special pride in her appearance, especially now that she and her beloved husband, Jason, were expecting their first child.

Her hand went lovingly to her stomach. A slight curve was starting to form—enough to let her know that Jason, Jr., was really there. She smiled at how adamant Jason was that this baby would be a son. "Of course it will be a son," Lillie thought aloud. "The Philips always get what they want."

At eighteen, Lillie Philips was the envy of many women in her hometown of Topeka, Kansas. She was considered one of Topeka's most beautiful women, with finely chiseled features that resembled a china doll. She had lived a spoiled and pampered life and enjoyed all the things money could buy. While other people put their faith and future in dreams and lofty aspirations, Lillie Philips had already come into her era of prosperity.

Lillie reached down and picked up an ornately framed picture of her best friend, Maggie Intissar. "No," she thought aloud. "Maggie Lucas." She and Maggie had shared many secrets and girlhood hopes together. When Maggie had lost her mother and brother in death and her father had deserted her to her grandmother's care, Lillie had helped Maggie through the pain. They were nearly inseparable, and when Lillie's family had chosen to build a home in the newly developed Potwin Place, Maggie's grandmother had agreed to have a home built next door so that Maggie and Lillie could continue to grow up together.

Lillie could scarcely believe that over seven months had passed since Maggie had been whisked away to her father's ranch in New Mexico by the dashing, mysterious Garrett Lucas.

Although Lillie knew that Maggie had hated her father at one time, she was happy Maggie had come to love him before his death. At least Maggie wouldn't have to carry that burden through life.

Lillie was grateful, too, that Maggie wouldn't have to be alone anymore. She was now Garrett Lucas's wife, and judging from the letters she sent to Lillie, Maggie was most content with the way her life had turned out.

Lillie smiled lovingly at the tintype. "Oh, Maggie," she sighed in contentment, "I can only hope that you're as happy as I am."

Hearing a carriage below on the cobblestone drive, Lillie forgot the picture and went quickly to the large cheval glass. She smoothed the lines of her blue, watered-silk, day dress that matched her eyes. It was the third gown she'd had on that day, and within the hour she'd dress again for dinner. Lillie couldn't get enough of rich, beautiful clothes and finery. She twirled in front of the mirror, making certain that every inch of the gown fell perfectly into place.

When she heard Jason's voice in the vestibule, Lillie quickly pinched her cheeks and fluffed the leg-of-mutton sleeves, lavishly created from expensive french lace. Finally satisfied with her appearance, Lillie descended the stairs in grand fashion to greet her husband.

Jason stood at the entryway table studying the day's mail. He lifted his gaze momentarily to catch sight of Lillie. Her beauty never failed to make him catch his breath.

The mail was quickly discarded as Lillie's satin-slippered feet reached the final step. Jason swept her into his arms and kissed her.

"Good evening, wife," he murmured affectionately.

"And good evening to you my beloved husband."

"Umm," Jason sighed against his wife's perfumed neck. "I've missed you today." Lillie relished the attention. It was hard to believe that they'd been married for nearly six months.

"Why don't we take our supper upstairs," Jason suggested.

Lillie felt shivers run down her spine. How she loved this romantic man! "I think it's a wonderful idea. I'll tell Cookie, and you go ahead upstairs." Jason smiled but refused to unhand Lillie.

"I need just one more kiss to see me through." Before Lillie could protest, Jason planted his lips firmly on hers.

"Perhaps," Lillie said, pulling away breathless from her husband's kiss, "we should forget supper and spend the evening curled up together in front of the fire."

Jason laughed heartily and set Lillie at arm's length. "Nonsense woman! I've worked a hard day at the law firm. In fact, I'll have you know that you're looking at a full partner in the law firm of Canton, Meiers, Johnston, and Philips.

"Oh Jason!" Lillie exclaimed. "Why didn't you tell me sooner? This is wonderful news. It's exactly what we'd hoped for. I'm so proud of you!" Lillie threw her arms around Jason's neck and hugged him tightly.

For the first time, Jason seemed to become aware of Lillie's rounding figure. His hand went to her still slender form and lovingly rested on the slight swelling. "I see my son is getting bigger each day."

"My daughter, you mean," Lillie couldn't help but tease.

"If you dare to have a daughter, my dear wife, I'm afraid I shall have to put you from the house!" With that Jason laughed good-naturedly, as did Lillie. Life was good, and they both knew how fortunate they'd been to be born to wealth and security.

An hour later the housekeeper appeared at Jason and Lillie's bedroom suite. She entered the sitting room carrying an overflowing tray of Cookie's finest culinary treats.

"Thank you very much, Mrs. Gregory," Lillie stated in a refined manner. "You may put it there," she motioned to the doily covered, Queen Ann table that stood beside the door.

Mrs. Gregory nodded and placed the tray on the table. "Will you be requiring my services for anything else, ma'am?" she requested in a formal, sedate fashion.

"I think not, Mrs. G.," Jason said as he emerged from the bedroom. "Lillie and I are celebrating, and we can do quite well on our own."

Mrs. Gregory gave a stiff nod and took her leave.

"Now, my dear," Jason said with a mischievous grin. "I think it time that you take down your hair and change into something more appropriate."

Lillie raised an eyebrow in mocking shock. "Why Jason

Philips, are you trying to romance me?"

Jason laughed aloud at this. "Trying? No. Succeeding? Yes. Now do you need my help?"

Lillie laughed softly. "No, no. I'll be back in a minute. You see to our supper."

Several days later, Lillie thought back to that evening as nearly the most perfect one of her marriage. Jason had looked so handsome, and he'd been so attentive. Then of course there was the promotion and the excitement of planning what they would do with the extra money that would soon be coming their way.

To match everything else, Lillie felt the baby move for the first time. Even Jason, Jr., wanted to be an important part of the celebration, Lillie remembered fondly. She was so anxious to have her baby and give him every benefit that life could afford. Her son, Lillie decided, would have the world at his feet; she'd see to that.

Lillie tapped her pen impatiently as she tried to keep her mind on the task at hand. She needed to decide which parties she and Jason would attend for the upcoming Christmas season and which they would decline.

She would have loved to attend them all, but that would be impossible. Not only were several of the galas being held on the same night, but propriety required that Lillie limit her public appearances.

In her growing condition, she felt it would be the height of bad taste to make her presence too obvious. Many people, especially the women, would talk behind her back for making any appearance at all, but Lillie was not about to miss the Christmas social season.

Several hours later, Lillie sat with a stack of rejected

invitations in one pile, acceptable events in another, and personalized, perfumed responses in yet another. Deciding to take a nap, Lillie rang a bell for Stanford, their household butler.

At Stanford's appearance, Lillie handed him her responses. "Would you see to it that these get posted. I'm going to take a short rest."

"Very good, Madam," Stanford said with a bow.

Lillie found the warmth of her downy quilts a comfort as she snuggled down deep into their folds. Outside, she could hear the wind blowing unmercifully against the window pane. It made a sad moaning sound leaving Lillie lonely as she faded into sleep.

Lillie knew that she was dreaming, but she felt a dread and fear that she'd never before known. She found herself in a small room. It was dark, and the air was stale and tainted by something foul. She struggled to find a way out of the room, and yet no aid to escape would show itself to her. Where was she?

The dream continued despite Lillie's fight to wake up. She was walking down a long corridor, and at a distance, a single candle was burning. As Lillie made her way to the candle, a draft blew out the flame. All at once, Lillie felt as if something cold and evil was upon her. She started to run, but the presence followed close behind her. Suddenly Lillie could feel its cold, icy breath on her neck.

With a start, Lillie sat straight up in bed. She'd never been one to have nightmares. Where had all those depressing images come from? She tried to laugh the dream off as the result of something she'd eaten, but in her heart, Lillie was troubled. She considered sharing her troubled thoughts with Jason but decided against it. Jason had been acting strained lately, and she didn't want to burden him further. Still, the dream was disturbing.

When Jason arrived home, Lillie was downstairs waiting to greet him at the door. When he entered the house, Lillie immediately perceived that something was troubling her young husband.

As Stanford took Jason's snow-covered outer coat, Lillie pulled her husband along with her to the front sitting room. A warm, cheery fire was blazing, and Lillie led Jason to a chair in front of it.

Jason refused, however, and took a seat instead on the red velvet sofa, pulling Lillie to sit beside him.

"But I was going to rub your neck," Lillie protested.

"It'll wait. Please sit with me," Jason said thoughtfully.

"What is it, Jason? You haven't quite seemed yourself since your promotion."

"That's what I want to talk about, Lillie. Do you know who Mr. Canton is?"

"He's the senior partner of the law firm, isn't he?"

"That's right. He had a long talk with me the day he promoted me." Lillie listened patiently as Jason continued. "I know this will sound strange, but Lillie, he wanted to talk to me about God."

"God?" Lillie questioned curiously. "What ever would God have to do with your promotion?"

"That's what I wondered, but the fact was, Mr. Canton said he was worried about me," Jason stated rather blankly.

"Worried about you? But whatever for? You perform your job admirably. You've earned recognition through your work with the Santa Fe Railroad," Lillie argued. "Why, Colonel Holliday said—"

"Yes, yes, Mr. Canton knows all about that," Jason

interrupted. "Surprisingly he knows a great deal about me."

"Then what is this about you and God?" Lillie questioned again.

"Mr. Canton told me that money could buy certain things in life, but it couldn't buy you life. Then he went on to explain that God was the only One Who could make life worth living," Jason answered.

"How did he propose God could do this?" Lillie inquired sarcastically.

"Now, Lil, just listen for a minute. Mr. Canton made a lot of sense that day. He made so much sense that I went back and talked to him again today."

Lillie moved away in shocked dismay. "Jason Philips, whatever on earth possessed you to do such a thing?"

"Because I realized that some of what he said made sense. There is an emptiness inside me. I hadn't thought about it much because every time I started to ponder the void, I'd find something else with which to occupy myself," Jason said reaching his hand out to Lillie.

Lillie surprised both of them by pulling away. "Jason, don't tell me you've found religion." She studied Jason's face. He paled slightly and a look of pain crossed his brow.

"I might as well be straight with you. I asked Mr. Canton how a person should go about having the special kind of relationship with God that he'd told me about. He told me that I needed to repent of my sins and ask Jesus Christ to be my Savior."

"And?" Lillie interrupted.

"And I did it. I asked Jesus into my heart. I'm a Christian now, Lillie."

"Oh, it's just that simple is it?" Lillie said with a hint of anger. "What kind of price tag comes with it?"

"What do you mean, Lillie?"

"Just how much of our hard-earned money is now designated to go to God?"

"It's hasn't got anything to do with money, Lillie. It has to do with your soul and where you'll spend eternity. It has to do with realizing that we are sinful and without Jesus Christ, that we can't hope to buy our way into heaven. I've accepted this way of life, Lillie. I'm not going to change my mind," Jason added softly.

Nothing could have shocked Lillie any more than Jason's announcement. She sat back against the sofa looking much like she'd had the wind knocked out of her.

When she could think rationally again, she questioned, "How does this affect us?"

Jason smiled. "That's what I wanted to talk to you about. Lillie, you need Jesus, too."

"I don't need religion, Jason Philips. Religion is for the poor in purse and poor in spirit. The two go hand in hand; they always have."

It was Jason's turn to look shocked. "Why Lillie Philips, what a snob you've become."

Lillie turned an indignant crimson. "How dare you! You've changed all our plans with one stroke of divine genius, and you call me names?" She stood up abruptly and started to walk from the room.

Jason was beside her in a flash. His wavy blond hair fell over one eye as he reached out to pull Lillie into his arms. "I didn't mean it Lillie. It's just that you sounded so, so different." Lillie refused to look at him, so Jason lifted her face with his hand.

"I love you, Lillie. That hasn't changed." Lillie softened

at his sad, boyish face. Jason was clearly suffering.

"I know you love me, Jason. But I don't think I can play second fiddle to God. That's not part of the dream we shared when you proposed. I don't mind if you have religion—after all we do attend church every Sunday—but please don't preach at me," Lillie said in a controlled, emotionless voice.

"I didn't mean to preach. I just got caught up in the moment. Finding God has been the best thing that's ever happened to me," Jason expressed enthusiastically.

"You used to say that about me," Lillie said stiffly as she pulled away from her husband. "Many wives have to contend with another woman, but I have to compete with God. Now I wonder, Jason Philips, which one of us do you think will win?"

Without waiting for an answer, Lillie swept from the room with the taffeta skirts of her evening gown rustling mockingly behind her.

two

Lillie passed through the next few days hostile and wounded. She barely spoke to Jason, and the loss was painfully evident in both of their lives. Every time her hand fell to her to stomach, Lillie felt like crying. How could things have gotten so far out of hand?

The things that normally cheered Lillie now had little effect. The Christmas tree had been put up in the front sitting room, and Lillie had gone Christmas shopping twice. Both times she'd come home with the carriage full of Christmas purchases, but the aching and loneliness wouldn't leave her. The place in her heart she'd reserved for Jason and their love seemed void of life.

The more Lillie tried to pretend that everything was all right, the worse things got. Jason was clearly in pain, and part of Lillie wanted to comfort him and tell him she would try his God. The other part of her was furious with both Jason and God for daring to change her plans and dreams.

On the Friday before Christmas, Lillie dressed with special care for the biggest gala of the Christmas season. The Cyrus Hollidays were throwing a party and had invited all of Topeka's elite. Lillie had nearly burst with pride at being included for such an occasion.

Lillie studied her appearance in the mirror. She'd had her figure corsetted as tightly as she dared. As a result, her stately hourglass figure showed little sign of her condition. Lillie admired the white velvet ball gown that she'd had specially made for the Hollidays' party.

Mrs. Gibson, her regular seamstress, had outdone herself, Lillie decided. The gown was generously designed with seventeen yards of the whitest velvet available. Mrs. Gibson had added red velvet ribbons to trim the skirt, bodice, and long, fitted sleeves. The bodice, though lower than Lillie would have liked, was lavishly trimmed in handmade Chantilly lace.

Turning ever so slightly, Lillie could admire the fashionable bustle bedecked in its trimmings. A huge red velvet bow lay across the top of the bustle and fell gracefully into the lavish folds of the gown. There had never been such a gown in all Kansas, Lillie decided self-confidently.

Noting the time, Lillie quickly secured a strand of pearls at her throat. Grabbing her matching velvet handbag, she made her way downstairs.

Jason was waiting in his study, and when Lillie appeared in the doorway he felt as if he'd been knocked down by a runaway train.

"Lillie, you are, without a doubt, the most beautiful woman in the world." His voice was deep and husky. Lillie maintained an aloofness that sent cold chills through Jason.

"Are you ready?" she questioned, knowing full well that he was. His own richly cut, black dinner jacket had a small snip of holly and ivy as a boutonniere. Jason was always thinking of clever things that way. Lillie hated to admit that her first impulse had been to throw herself into his arms.

"I'm ready, but there is something I'd like to give you before we leave," Jason said softly as he crossed the room to stand before Lillie.

"Give me?" Lillie questioned, knowing that her abominable behavior of the last few days had not merited any generosity.

"I wasn't sure if you'd like it, but I hope you do. It's my peace offering."

Lillie took the small box. Obviously jewelry, she judged. She opened the box and gasped. A diamond and ruby necklace with accompanying earrings lay glittering up at her.

"Oh, Jason, how wonderful!" Lillie said as she lifted the necklace up to catch the light. "Help me put it on," she requested as she undid the clasp on her pearls.

Jason smiled sadly. "It's nice to know that I can still do something to please you," he answered as he secured the necklace. Lillie immediately took pity on him.

"Oh, Jason," she fairly purred. "I'm sorry for the way I've acted. I didn't know what to think. I thought maybe you would stop loving me."

Jason pulled Lillie into his arms. "I could never stop loving you. You are an important part of my life." He bent his head to kiss her, and when Lillie didn't stiffen or pull away, Jason kissed her long and passionately.

Lillie's arms went around her husband's neck. How she had missed him and his kisses. She vowed then and there to put aside her differences and be a loving wife to Jason.

At the sound of Stanford clearing his throat, Jason released Lillie with a gleam of sheer ecstacy in his expression.

"Yes, Stanford?" Jason asked nonchalantly. Lillie took this opportunity to replace her earrings with the diamond and ruby ones. She was admiring the effect in the mirror when she overheard the butler speak.

"Sir, it's begun to sleet. I've taken the liberty of bringing the carriage to the side entrance."

"Very good, Stanford," Jason replied and turned to assist Lillie.

Jason handed Lillie into the carriage and climbed up beside her. After tucking a blanket around them both, he tapped on the carriage top to signal the driver that they were ready.

"You know, Lillie, I've been thinking that after the baby comes, perhaps we could take a trip to Chicago. I know there are some things for the house that you've been wanting to buy. What do you think?"

Lillie could barely see her husband's face in the shadows of the carriage, but she could tell he was smiling. "What a wonderful idea, Jason. Is this another Christmas present?"

"In a way. I thought that you might like to do something different after our son's birth. I know that from here on out you'll be rather confined, and I wanted to give you something to look forward to in the spring beside croquet."

Lillie laughed at Jason's reference to her favorite lawn game. "Well you most certainly have," she said and leaned over to kiss Jason's cheek. The carriage jostled her, however, and she found herself thrown against his shoulder instead.

"Jones?" Jason called out the window to the driver as the carriage again lurched to the right. "What's wrong?"

"Ice, sir. My apologies but I'm doing everything I can."

A sickening cold penetrated Lillie's bones. There was something about the darkness and the cold that reminded her of the nightmare she'd had. She tried to shake off the feeling as she braced herself against the rocking of the carriage, but it wouldn't leave. The stab of her tightly laced, whalebone corset, made her cry out.

"Are you all right?" Jason questioned, pulling Lillie close to keep her from bouncing around the inside of the carriage.

"I am now," Lillie whispered. "Please just hold me."

Lillie relished Jason's embrace, but her uneasiness continued to mount. She could hear the driver fighting the horses.

"Lillie did you hear me? Should we turn back? I mean, I'd hate to miss the party, but your welfare is more important to me." Jason's tone betrayed his concern.

Lillie straightened up in surprise. "No! I don't want to miss the Hollidays' party. I could miss all the other festivities, but not this one."

The carriage again slid sideways and Jason grabbed the side with his free hand. "I don't know. I think we should go home." The clatter of the carriage wheels on wood, made Jason realize they'd reached one of two creek crossings that lay between their home and the Holliday residence.

Lillie patted Jason's hand. "See silly, we're nearly there. That was the first of the Twin Bridges. The second should be just ahead, and then we're only a few blocks away."

"Yes, I know," Jason said, but he didn't sound reassured.

Lillie and Jason startled at the sound of the horses' nervous whinnies. The driver was urging the animals forward, but something had frightened the thoroughbreds. The wagon pitched forward, sliding sharply to the left and then to the right.

The horses sounded again, but this time in a desperate cry. As the carriage began to cross the second of the two bridges, the horses faltered and stopped. The driver got down from the carriage to pull the animals across the bridge. The unexpected movement beside the horses startled them, and they tried first to rear up, and then to back away from the driver.

Lillie panicked when she heard the first sickening sound of wood breaking. Jason was reaching for the door when the carriage pushed through the wooden railing and the back wheel slid off the bridge.

"Just sit still, Lillie," Jason ordered.

For several minutes nothing seemed to happen. After that, however, everything happened at once. Lillie was gripping the side of the carriage, her heart pounding with fear. Choking back tears, Lillie recognized her nightmare.

Jason was calling out to Jones and opening the carriage door when the back end of the carriage went off the bridge. The bottom of the carriage hit with a loud thud that sent Jason to the floor, half in the carriage, half out. Lillie reached forward to help her husband.

"Jason, give me your hand," she tried to sound calm, but her words resembled hysteria.

Jason was dazed for a moment, and then reached back to take Lillie's offered hand. Thinking better of it, however, he waved her away. The horses were fighting the pull of the carriage against their harnesses, while Jones was still working to get them to pull forward.

"Lillie, listen to me," Jason began. "We've got to get out of here. I want you to move slowly to the other side of the carriage. Can you do that?"

Lillie nodded. "I think so." Her voice sounded much

calmer. "Jason," she continued, "I love you. Please tell me everything will be all right."

The carriage lurched again. They were losing ground fast. The body of the carriage slipped farther backward. They were now at such an angle that Lillie could see the surface of the bridge through the carriage door window.

"Lillie," Jason reached for his wife. How could he tell her of the fear in his heart? How could he explain the imminent danger they were in? "Lillie, will you pray with me?"

"Pray?" Lillie gasped the question. "Pray at a time like this. Jason we've got to get out of here or we'll go over the side with the carriage."

Jason's face was barely illuminated by the faint glow of street lights. Lillie saw anguish fill his eyes. Suddenly she felt the carriage move, and she knew that they were going over the edge.

"I love you, Lillie," were the last words Jason spoke.

"Jason!" Lillie screamed. Then amidst the noise of screaming horses and splintering wood, Lillie's head hit something hard, and she lost consciousness.

Lillie was lost in her nightmare again. She felt the bone-chilling cold and knew the darkness would never turn to light. She thought several times that someone was calling to her. Other times she heard crying. Where was she and why couldn't she make herself wake up? Lillie felt frightened for the first time in her life.

Lillie forced herself to open her eyes. The room was dark, except for a ribbon of light that came in through the partially opened door.

Lillie tried to sit up but was stopped by a sharp stab of pain. "Help me!" she screamed. "Somebody help me, please!" She was nearly hysterical when a nurse entered the room.

"There, there," the woman said, patting Lillie's hand and pushing the hair back from her face.

"Where am I? What's wrong with me?" Lillie sobbed.

"You're in the hospital. Don't you remember the accident?"

The accident? Yes, Lillie did remember. The whole ugly scene passed before her eyes again. The carriage, Jason's sad smile. Jason!

"Where's my husband? Where is Jason?" Lillie questioned the nurse.

The woman paled slightly and moved to pour Lillie a drink of water. "I think you'd better rest for a few moments. I need to get the doctor."

Lillie refused the water and grabbed the woman's hand. "Where is my husband?" She longed for the answer, yet in her heart she knew that the news was not good.

"I'm sorry, miss." The woman was nearly in tears. "Your husband was killed in the accident."

Lillie heard someone screaming and then realized that she was making the noise. She raged against the bed that held her captive and, blind to the pain, tried to sit up. "I want Jason! I want my husband!"

Just then another nurse entered the room with a doctor closely behind her. "What's all this commotion?" the doctor bellowed, and Lillie immediately calmed.

"Where's my husband? That woman said he's dead. Please tell me she's lying!" Lillie begged the doctor.

"Just relax and lie back. I need to examine you. Do you realize how long you've been unconscious?" The doctor acted as though he'd not heard Lillie's questions. He worked quickly to take Lillie's mind off her fears.

"I...I don't know," Lillie stammered. "It seems like just yesterday."

"Well you gave us quite a fright. We weren't sure you'd ever wake up again," the doctor answered. "Now just follow my finger with your eyes. No, don't move your head."

Lillie did as he asked, but her mind wouldn't let the questions be dismissed. "How long have I been unconscious?"

"Two weeks. Today is New Year's Day."

"New Year's? But it was the week before Christmas. Jason and I...." Lillie's words trailed off. "Jason is dead?"

"I'm sorry," the doctor whispered, and Lillie could see the emotion in his eyes.

"How?" she whispered the question.

"He died instantly in the accident," the doctor replied and added, "He didn't suffer."

Lillie felt tears stream down her face. Her hand went to her abdomen as it had so often after learning of her condition. There was no rounding, and Lillie knew that she'd lost her child.

"My baby is gone," she announced as if the doctor and his nurses would find this news.

"Yes," the doctor said softly. Lillie saw tears in the eyes of the nurses.

"I'd like to be alone," she said, turning her face away. The doctor nodded and ushered the nurses from the room.

three

Two months later, Lillie sat in the parlor of her parent's Potwin Place home. They had brought her there from the hospital, and she'd taken residence in her old bedroom on the third floor. She was awaiting a meeting with her in-laws and the lawyer that handled the family business.

It was the first time Lillie had agreed to see anyone outside of her family, and she was very nervous about the meeting. She smoothed her unadorned black dress and sighed. She had gained over thirty pounds in the last months and although unhappy about it, Lillie had done nothing to prevent it. She'd taken on a lifestyle of solitary hours with boxes of chocolates at her fingertips.

At the sound of voices in the hallway, Lillie stiffened.

"Lillie, they're here." Grace Johnston looked more haggard than Lillie could remember. Lillie nodded to her mother and moved to the window seat.

Grace stepped away from the door and returned with their guests.

"Lillie, dear." It was Gladys Philips. She swept across the room and noted the lack of color in Lillie's face and the added weight. "Jason wouldn't want you to suffer so." Lillie nodded. She knew it was true but had no response to offer.

Her father-in-law, John Philips, stood behind his wife. He smiled slightly, reminding Lillie of Jason's sad little smiles. Why did she have to hurt like this? Why couldn't she have died, too?

The other man cleared his voice. All eyes turned to greet Stanley Canton. Lillie acknowledged him with a nod but said nothing.

"We might as well get to the business at hand," Mr. Canton was beginning. He greeted Lillie's father who had just entered the room and taken a seat by Grace. John and Gladys Philips also took their seats and awaited Mr. Canton's announcement.

"Mrs. Philips," Mr. Canton spoke to Lillie with genuine kindness in his voice. "Your husband was a dear friend and colleague. I extend my deepest sympathies to you."

"Thank you," Lillie answered mechanically.

"To make this as short and painless as possible," Mr. Canton continued, "You're a wealthy young woman, Mrs. Philips. Jason's will entitles you to everything. An account has been set up in your name at the bank, and funds will be transferred there for your use. If there is anything I can do for you, please feel free to call upon me."

All eyes were on her, and Lillie suddenly longed for the sanctuary of her bedroom. She knew that she was expected to say something, but what was there to say?

Seeing her hesitation, Mr. Canton tried to offer what he felt would be comfort. "Mrs. Philips your husband and baby are safely in heaven. You will see them again."

Sudden rage filled Lillie. Standing to her feet, she lashed out at her husband's friend. "I'll have no part of a God Who would rob a woman of her husband and child. A God Who cares not one whit for the pain I am suffering and the devastation that I shall have to go through life experiencing."

Lillie ignored the gasps of surprise from Gladys. She

knew that her in-laws were Christians and held God's will in the highest esteem.

"This shouldn't surprise anyone. It's you who surprise me. How you can all sit there so calm, so resigned! Well I'm not resigned. I shall never give myself over to the will of an unmerciful God. If Jason's God wants Jason and our baby, then so be it. But He'll not have my gracious consent, nor my heart!" With that, Lillie walked from the room and ran up the stairs to her bedroom.

She threw herself, breathless, across the bed, and cried tears of anger and sorrow. She heard someone enter the room, and when her mother pulled her into her arms, Lillie allowed it.

"Lillie, you're so distraught. Is there anything I can do to help?" Her mother's voice was soothing. Lillie felt as if she were a little girl again. How she wished she could be a child once more!

"Oh, Mother, I hurt so much. I can scarcely breathe for the pain that binds me. How can I live without him? How can I wake up in the morning and know that I'll never hear his laughter again, never hear his voice nor feel his touch?" Lillie's tears flowed freely, while Grace Johnston continued to hold her daughter. "And, my baby. My dear, sweet little baby." The heart wrenching sobs were almost more than Grace could stand.

"Go ahead Lillie, just get it all out. All the pain and bitterness," Lillie's mother stroked her daughter's hair.

"What am I to do Mother?" Lillie questioned, trying to dry her face.

Grace Johnston looked deep into her daughter's red-rimmed eyes. She wanted so much to help her child. An idea came to her. "Lillie, you need a place to heal. I think you should go and stay with Maggie for a time. She loves you so much and has offered several times to have you recuperate at her ranch."

Lillie thought the matter over for a moment. Perhaps her mother was right. Maggie's letters had told of a glorious mountain valley where her father had built a cattle empire. Maggie made the place sound nearly perfect. Maybe she should go, Lillie reasoned. Perhaps the drier climate would offer a welcomed change from the damp, cold of Topeka's spring weather.

"Yes, Mother. I think it would be a wonderful idea," Lillie finally answered.

"Good. I'll speak with your father and have him make all the arrangements," Grace said as she stood. "Now, you start packing. And Lillie," she paused at the doorway. "I think it might be nice if you took something other than black. Jason wouldn't want you to mourn. Forget about society. No one at Maggie's ranch is going to care."

"I'll think about it, Mother."

By the second week in April, Lillie was in the private train car of a man her family fondly called Uncle William. The man, in truth, was William Strong, president of the Atchison, Topeka, and Santa Fe Railroad.

Lillie had grown up knowing Uncle William as intimately as she had any family member, even though he had no blood tie to her family. When William Strong learned that Lillie was to travel to New Mexico, he wouldn't hear of her doing it any other way than by his private car.

Once the train was well out of Topeka, Lillie removed her black hat and veil. She smoothed back her blond hair and sat back against the plush velvet seat.

She was traveling in grand style thanks to Uncle William. From the floor to the chair railing, the sitting room of the train car was richly paneled in walnut. Above this was a red velvet, fleur-de-lis-patterned wallpaper, with a tiny gold ribbon running vertically.

Lillie sat in silence trying to take in her surroundings. She glanced down at her plump figure and sighed. The worse she felt about her appearance, the more she ate. It was like trying to fill a void that couldn't be filled. She'd packed four boxes of bonbons to bring with her on the trip to Maggie's.

When night fell, Lillie went into the bedroom. Pulling the black bombazine dress over her head, she quickly replaced it with a flowing, white flannel nightgown and for a moment, the contrast seemed strangely significant. Black and white; good and evil; dead and alive.

She thought for a time of Jason and his words about God. Then the words that Mr. Canton had shared came back to haunt her. God had taken all that she loved. How could she love Him after that? Why should she? She had enough money to do whatever she wanted. She didn't need anything or anyone, especially God.

The gentle rocking of the train lulled Lillie to sleep, and for once, the nightmare didn't wake her up screaming. Instead, she found herself in pleasant memories of Jason and their baby. When she awoke, she ached at the reality that those memories were only a dream. Lillie hugged her knees to her chest and cried.

The solitude of the private car had its drawbacks, and Lillie soon discovered that with other people around she hadn't been given to thinking constantly about her pain.

She walked around the room, gingerly testing her balance against the rocking and swaying of the train car.

After she dressed, Lillie went to the mirror and grimaced at her reflection. Her face was puffy and blotched from crying. It nearly made her want to put the veiled hat back on.

Instead, Lillie looked out the windows and was surprised to find the train slowing to a stop. She went from one side of the car to the other, and finding nothing but rolling prairie, Lillie began to fear train robbers or something worse.

She jumped in nervous surprise when a loud pounding sounded at her car door. Suspiciously she opened it and found the train conductor standing before her.

"Pardon me, ma'am, but we have an emergency," he said doffing his cap in respect.

"What is it that you expect me to do about it?" Lillie questioned rather rudely.

"There's a young woman in the train car up ahead. She's about to give birth, and the young doctor helping her needs a place to deliver her child."

Lillie felt as if a knife had been plunged into her heart. Her child would have been due this month, a point that she had struggled to forget. How dare God do this to her? How could He be so heartless as to force her to face it all again?

"I'm sorry, you can't use my car," Lillie said and fairly pushed the conductor back through the doorway. She slammed the door in his face and put her face in her hands.

Lillie had just taken a seat when the door flew open with a loud crash. Filling the door was a handsome, blond man who painfully reminded Lillie of Jason. He was furious, and his eyes burned holes into Lillie.

"How dare you deny someone the right to proper care! You have more than enough space here, and we would only be here long enough to get to the next town. What kind of heartless woman are you?"

Lillie felt bile in her throat. She felt her face turn crimson under the man's merciless scrutiny. "I. . .I," she stammered to say something, to fight back, but no words would come.

"I don't care what you think or what you say, but I have instructed several men to bring that woman here. I shall bind you to your chair if you object, but she will deliver her baby here!" With that he turned and motioned the others to enter the room.

Lillie sat frozen to her chair. She watched as the young doctor cleared the table and had the woman placed on it. Her car had become a flurry of activities, all amidst the cries and screams of the young woman.

Watching the woman's swollen abdomen heave with each contraction, Lillie could no longer remain. She rushed from the car into the prairie fields. She ran and ran, until her breath refused to come. She was mindless of her steps and had no idea where she was. Gasping, Lillie fell to the ground. The springtime smells of rich dirt and new wheat assaulted Lillie's nose.

It didn't matter that she was face down in the dirt. Lillie no longer cared. She cried and cried until she felt certain she could cry no more, but the tears refused to abate. She had no idea how long she lay there, but all at once someone was lifting her.

She opened her eyes to find the concerned blue gray eyes of the angry doctor. He was cradling her against his chest and hushing her tears. Lillie relaxed despite wanting nothing of his comfort.

When her breathing was less ragged and the tears had

been wiped from her eyes, Lillie looked up as if to question the stranger who held her.

"I'm Dr. Monroe. Dr. Daniel Monroe," he said as if anticipating her question. "I'm sorry to have treated you so harshly. I can see that you're in mourning."

Lillie found herself touched by his concern. It was the first time since Jason's death that she'd felt anything but the pain and numbness that had haunted her every waking moment.

"I'm Lillie Phil…," she choked on the word. "I'm Lillie, Dr. Monroe," she finally offered.

"Call me Daniel." His words were gentle, almost tender.

Lillie stiffened slightly. She didn't desire that kind of familiarity, but it seemed quite awkward calling him Dr. Monroe. Maybe she wouldn't have to call him by any name at all. "How is your patient—your patients?" Lillie questioned.

A frown crossed Daniel's face and anger again filled his eyes. "They're dead."

Lillie felt her chest tighten. The young mother and her child were dead. Dead! Dead! Dead! The word reverberated through Lillie's mind.

She struggled to draw a deep breath. It was like that moment in the hospital when she had to face up to losing Jason and their baby. Why was this happening again?

"You don't look at all well, Lillie," Daniel said, noticing that the woman in his arms had paled considerably. "I think I'd better get you back to the train so you can lie down."

Lillie nodded and allowed Daniel to lead her back to the train. Looking around her for the first time, Lillie realized they were quite a distance from the train and the ground around them was rough and uneven. Taking a step gingerly, Lillie nearly tripped as what looked like solid ground gave way to dust. She grimaced when Daniel's hand tightened upon her arm, but she said nothing.

When Daniel and Lillie entered the private car, the conductor quickly joined them. "We've made arrangements for the woman and her baby. I'm sorry, but I need to get this train back on schedule."

Daniel nodded. "I'm going to stay with this young woman. She's not feeling well and needs my attention." Lillie started to protest, but she was too tired. She was very faint.

"Thanks, Doc," the conductor was saying. "Thanks for all you did. That little gal gave it all she had."

"Yes, she did," Daniel said, and Lillie noticed how his voice was void of feeling. What manner of man was this Dr. Daniel Monroe?

Proprieties seemed unimportant, and as the train was once again underway, Lillie tolerated Daniel's attentions. She watched him curiously. He was about six inches taller than she, and the way his sandy blond hair fell over one eye reminded her of Jason. After taking Lillie's pulse and temperature, Daniel ordered her to lie down and take a nap. To his surprise, Lillie didn't argue.

As Daniel took hold of Lillie's waist to steady her walk, he saw the pained expression in her eyes. His touch was grieving her. "Your husband?" he questioned, and Lillie knew that he referred to her mourning.

"Yes. We were in a carriage accident," Lillie murmured. It suddenly seemed important to explain her earlier harshness. "I also lost my baby. He would have been born this month."

It was now Daniel's face that held the pained expression. He felt the old anger returning. He stopped beside the bedroom compartment door. "I am so sorry, Lillie. How calloused you must have thought me. How stupid I am."

Lillie was amazed at the fury he seemed to vent upon himself. "You had no way of knowing," she whispered.

"There seems to be a great deal I don't know," Daniel said and his ominous tone caused Lillie to take a step back. "Otherwise, that woman and her child wouldn't have died!" Then he left, closing the bedroom door behind him.

four

Lillie slept soundly for several hours, but as if on cue, the nightmares started again. She tossed from one side of the bed to the other in a vain search for comfort. She saw the same shadows and felt the same numbing cold. She was searching down a long corridor for her crying baby. When at last she came to a door where the crying sounded loudest, she tried the knob. It was unmovable. Lillie cried softly as she listened to the baby cry.

Suddenly the dream changed. She was standing beside the young pregnant woman who'd died in her train car. The woman was crying out to Lillie for help, but as Lillie reached out the figure changed and it was Jason's face she saw.

"Lillie, wake up!" Lillie felt herself being roused into consciousness. She opened her eyes to see steely blue eyes staring down at her.

"Oh, Jason, I had the most terrible dream," she reached out to hold tightly to the man she thought was her husband.

"Lillie, it's Daniel." The words cut her as surely as if they'd been a knife. The nightmare had been true.

Suddenly, Lillie pushed back as though she'd touched a red hot iron. "What are you doing here?"

"You were crying and screaming," Daniel tried to answer in a soothing tone.

"And?" Lillie refused to be comforted.

Daniel stood up and narrowed his eyes. "And I ran in

from the sitting room to help you." he said indignantly and went from the room.

Lillie, fully cothed, followed him into the sitting room of the train car. She immediately went for a box of candy and sat down at the same table where Dr. Monroe's patient had died. The table had been cleaned, and the cloth and flowers replaced. Like everything else in Lillie's life, it appeared untouched by the loss.

Unaware that Daniel watched her, Lillie opened the box and began to eat chocolate after chocolate. She stared out into the darkness beyond her window. The only light in the compartment was that of a low burning lamp.

"You're going to make yourself sick," Daniel said as he took the seat across from Lillie.

"It's none of your concern," Lillie answered rudely.

"I see."

"I'm glad you do," Lillie replied. "I certainly don't need you telling me what to do."

"You must have been quite thin," he said with a mocking tone and added, "not so long ago."

"You're a very rude man to discuss a woman's figure, and how would you know whether I was fat or thin?" Lillie questioned.

"I figure at the rate you're eating those candies, you must have been thin. Otherwise you'd be much heavier now." Daniel's tone held amusement, and Lillie felt herself turn crimson at the words.

"You are, without a doubt, the rudest man I've ever met. If you're as poor a doctor as you are a gentleman, no wonder your patients die."

The words hit their mark, for Lillie saw a dark scowl cross Daniel's face. For several minutes no one said anything, and Lillie began to regret the tactless way she'd handled her embarrassment.

"I'm sorry. You are of course only speaking as a physician, and I am allowing my recent pain to affect my manners," Lillie apologized, not understanding why she felt the need to.

Daniel remained quiet. Lillie believed him to be contemplating the young woman who'd died in childbirth. It must be difficult to be a doctor and see death everyday, she thought.

In his mind, Daniel saw an angelic face contorted with pain. The young woman in his memories was slowly dying. Dying by trying to give life to a child: his child. His young wife hadn't lived, despite his efforts to deliver their baby. Their child had never been born, having gone to the grave with Katie Monroe.

Daniel shook off the memory and tried to concentrate on the face before him. "You are, of course, right," he said with more sadness to his voice than Lillie had ever heard from another human being. "I suppose I'm not much of a doctor. However, I do know that you are trying to eat away your grief, and it won't work. You're a fine looking woman, Lillie. Why let this continue?"

Getting to her feet, Lillie steadied her nerves with a deep breath. "I think it would be to both our benefits if you were to take your place with the other passengers. I'd like you to leave my train car at the next stop."

"Why wait?" Daniel questioned angrily, as he got to his feet and crossed the room. He pulled open the door and stepped out onto the boarding platform. With one fluid motion, he crossed the railings between the two cars and stood on the platform of the car that joined Lillie's private car to the rest of the train.

"I am sorry to have brought you more pain, Mrs. . . ." He paused, waiting for Lillie to respond. Lillie stood in shock. The noise of the train wheels and the grinding and pitching of the cars filled the room.

"Well, Lillie," he said in a rather sarcastic tone, "I bid you farewell. Enjoy your chocolates." With that, Daniel Monroe opened the door to the adjoining car and entered, slamming the door behind him.

Several hours later, Lillie stood, thinking, at the door of the car. Her curiosity drew her out onto the platform of the train car. The morning sun was starting to rise on the prairie horizon. The sky was filled with glorious red ribbons of color against the violet hue of dawn. Red sails in the morning, sailors take warning, Lillie thought.

She walked closer to the edge of the railing. Watching the ground pass beneath the train's couplings, Lillie gave serious thought to jumping off the train. She wanted to die. There was nothing left to live for. All that she loved was gone, and now she was making her way to her best friend, who was newly married and no doubt, very happy. How could she bear being surrounded by Maggie's joy?

Clacky, clack. Clacky, clack. The noise was hypnotic. Lillie gripped the rail tightly, searching her heart for a reason to go on. There was none.

In the connecting car, Daniel had just removed his coat and was turning in his seat when his eye got a glimpse of Lillie moving toward the rail.

He watched her stand there. She was watching the ground race past her, and Daniel knew that she was making a choice between life and death. He wouldn't allow her to choose death. He moved down the aisle and stood, hand on the door, ready to leap across the expanse and pull her back from the clutches of death if necessary.

Something inside him ached for this woman. She was so young, obviously well-to-do, and probably used to having everything her way. But somewhere along the way, she'd been told no, and her loss was more than she could bear. For reasons beyond his understanding, Daniel wanted to hold her and comfort her. It took all of his willpower to remain hidden behind the door.

Lillie stood for a long time. She thought about her life. What should she do? Death beckoned her, but something held her back. She thought of something Jason had once told her. She tried to remember each word, but all that came to mind was that Jason had tried to show her a verse in the Bible.

The spell of the rails was broken, and Lillie went back into the train car and searched for Uncle William's Bible. She knew that the highly religious William Strong would have a Bible somewhere on his private train car.

Daniel breathed a sigh of relief as he watched Lillie hurry into her car. The decision to live had been made, at least for the time being. He couldn't explain why that seemed important to him, but it was. Taking his seat, Daniel dozed off and on, blending memories of his long departed Katie with those of the mysterious woman whom he only knew as Lillie.

Lillie's search finally turned up a well-worn copy of the Bible. Thumbing through the many pages, Lillie finally recognized the Gospel of Luke as the one Jason had tried to share. Despair filled her as she realized she would have to read every verse in the Gospel of Luke to find Jason's verse.

After flipping several pages, Lillie's eyes fell upon Luke 12:19-21: "And I will say to my soul, Soul, thou hast much goods laid up for many years; take thine ease, eat, drink, and be merry. But God said unto him, Thou fool, this night thy soul shall be required of thee: then whose shall those things be, which thou hast provided? So is he that layeth up treasure for himself, and is not rich toward God." Lillie slammed the Bible shut.

Her body trembled from head to toe. How could Jason love such a God? Lillie's rage toward God began to build. Did God kill Jason because he hadn't given enough money to the church? Was this the reason she'd lost all that she loved?

Lillie paced the room despite the rocking of the car. What kind of God would take the life of an industrious young man simply because he didn't give enough money to the church? Lillie vowed never again to read the Bible. She replaced the book where she'd found it and went to bed.

It was well past noon when Lillie awoke. The train was strangely silent, and the rocking had stilled. She got up and washed her face. Looking at the wrinkled black dress, Lillie went to where her other gowns were hanging. At her mother's encouragement, Lillie had brought several dresses that hadn't been dyed black for mourning.

She ran a hand over the dark blue, calico, day dress that her mother had recently made for her. Lillie frowned, knowing that the reason for the new dresses had been her recent weight gain. Still, when Lillie thought of Jason she knew her mother was right. Jason would hate her wearing black. Even before he had become a Christian, he had detested the practice of months, even years, of mourning being practiced by young, vibrant people who deserved to go on living.

Lillie stared at the clothes for a few more minutes and made a decision. She would no longer wear widow's weeds. She would burn all the black clothing or at least throw it from the train as soon as they were traveling again.

She took a seat by the window, watching with disinterest the passing life of the small town. In a short time, the train was on its way, and only then did the thought cross Lillie's mind: she'd never notified Maggie that she was coming.

Lillie tried to think if her mother had said anything about sending Maggie a letter or telegram, and she soon realized that nothing had been said about such things.

After she considered her plight for a few moments, Lillie was shocked to find herself thinking back on Daniel Monroe. She remembered his boyish smile and sandy hair. His hair was wavy, where Jason's had been straight, but it was nearly the same color. It's only because he reminds me of Jason, Lillie thought. It's Jason, I really miss. It's his comforting I want.

Lillie felt guilty because of her thoughts of Daniel. Jason had only been gone a little more than three months. How could she be so callous as to give Dr. Monroe more than a fleeting thought?

"I'm a terrible person," Lillie said aloud. "I didn't deserve Jason, and that's why he's gone." Even in speaking the words, Lillie didn't believe them. It didn't make sense to think that way, and it wasn't the least bit comforting.

She rubbed her temples for a moment and realized that she still hadn't pinned up her hair. She let her hand run down the length of her long blond hair and cried. Jason had loved her hair. He was ever after her to let it down. She had thought him such a bother when he pulled at her hairpins, but she fervently wished he were here to play his troublesome game once more.

Without thinking, Lillie went to her sewing bag and pulled out her embroidery shears. Mindless that she'd never had a haircut in her life, Lillie began to cut her hair. She had to leave Jason's memory behind or go mad. She had to forget the past and every detail of her life before this moment.

Snip. . .snip. . .snip. The scissors found their mark, and within moments, Lillie was surrounded by a pile of honey-blond hair. She went to her bed compartment and studied her reflection in the mirror. Her hair fell in a blunt cut, just to the shoulders. It made her face seem thinner. Taking the scissors once more, Lillie deliberated her appearance and cut a framing edge of bangs to fall just above her eyebrows. Satisfied that she looked nothing like Jason's Lillie, she went back to the main compartment and gathered up the discarded hair.

When she opened the door to her car, Lillie was surprised at how dry the air seemed. Funny, she hadn't noticed it before. She stood holding her hair in her hands for a moment. "Jason," she whispered to the passing scenery, "I'll never love anyone again, but I can't think of you anymore." She took a handful of the hair and allowed the wind to catch it. Lillie watched as her hair drifted into the nearby field of sage grass. "Goodbye, beloved.

"And my precious baby," Lillie forced herself to say the words. "I would have loved you so dearly, but instead I must live without you. Goodbye, little angel," she said and cast the remaining golden hair to the wind.

It was a turning point, Lillie knew. She went back into the car and pulled down all the black dresses she'd brought with her. "No more mourning," she said as she returned to the train platform and threw the dresses into the open prairie field. She nearly laughed aloud to imagine someone coming along and finding long strands of blond hair and then black bombazine gowns.

The crisp, dry air felt good on her face, and Lillie shook out her shoulder length hair, running a hand through the strands just to get the feel of it. She felt freer than she had in months. "Goodbye, Lillie Philips," she whispered to the air. "From now on I'll just be Lillie."

From the adjoining car, Daniel watched quizzically at the performance that had taken place on the coupling platform. He was stunned to find that Lillie had cut her hair, although he had to admit he liked the new look. It was in total confusion that he watched her throw her clothes from the train, but Daniel knew what it was to say goodbye to the past.

Maybe Lillie had decided life was worth living after all, he thought. Maybe her performance signaled an end to her self-imposed destruction.

Daniel tried to think of his destination instead of Lillie, but the delicate face continued to haunt him. Who was she and why did he seem to care so much?

five

Maggie Lucas pulled back on the reins of her favorite horse. "Whoa, Thunder." She paused on the ridge high above Pinon Canyon Ranch. Below, she could see her husband, Garrett, working with several other men. They were mending fence. There were many things about ranch life that her husband loved, but mending fences wasn't one of them.

Thunder whinnied softly, bringing the attention of the men to the ridge. Garrett wiped the sweat from his forehead and squinted against the bright April sunlight. When he spied Maggie on the ridge, he smiled.

"I think it's time for me to ride ahead and see if there are any more spots we need to patch," Garrett said with a grin to his hard-working foreman.

"Sure, ride off and leave us with the dirty work," Mack Reynolds feigned the complaint. The fact was that this was the happiest he'd seen his boss in years. When Maggie's father had passed away the October before, Mack had worried that Garrett would sink into depression. He knew Garrett had lived long enough with Jason Intissar to consider him a father in every way that counted. But marriage to Maggie had left Garrett too preoccupied to grieve for long.

Mack turned to make a comment to Garrett, but his boss was already astride his horse, Alder, and headed towards his young wife.

"Well, you certainly took your sweet time getting here," Maggie said laughingly as Garrett reined up beside her.

"Come here," Garrett motioned with his index finger.

Maggie smiled broadly, "Make me." With that she kicked her heels into Thunder's side and left Garrett in the dust.

After months of riding this ridge, Maggie knew every rut and boulder. She steered Thunder away from dangerous places, even though Thunder, too, was well aware of the hazards. Maggie leaned flat against Thunder's neck as she heard Alder's thundering approach.

Garrett came up beside her and plucked Maggie easily from Thunder's back into his arms. He slowed Alder's pace and pulled Maggie tightly against him.

"Umm," Garrett whispered against her ear. "You smell wonderful."

"I've been baking bread. You're just hungry." Maggie smiled, put her arms around her husband's neck, and added, "But if you don't catch up with Thunder, you'll have no lunch."

"Maybe I'll just feast on you," Garrett whispered and nipped playfully at Maggie's neck. She squealed in laughing delight and shifted her weight, nearly sending them sideways off Alder.

"I think I'd better catch up with Thunder," Garrett laughed.

After Maggie was safely back on her horse, Garrett led her to a secluded oasis. "Oh Garrett, this is a beautiful spot. How come I've never found it?" Maggie asked as she slid down from her horse.

"It's a secret place reserved for people in love. Unless you're in love, you just can't find it," Garrett replied, taking the saddlebags from Maggie's horse.

"Then how come you knew about it for so long?" Maggie teased.

Garrett dropped the saddlebags and pulled Maggie into his arms. "Because, Magdelena Intissar Lucas, I've loved you since I first laid eyes on your father's portrait of you. That sassy, spitfire of a girl broke my heart so that I could love no other." With that, Garrett bent down and kissed Maggie long and passionately.

"I feel so blessed," she whispered as she walked with Garrett to a stand of tall cottonwood trees.

They spent most of the afternoon laughing and talking. They were still newlyweds as far as Maggie was concerned, having only been married for six months. It was upon that very reflection that Garrett suddenly brightened.

"Maggie, you know what I owe you?"

Maggie stared in bewilderment. "What could you possibly owe me?"

"A honeymoon. We never got away after the wedding. Of course, what with your pa's death," Garrett paused remembering how Maggie's father had pleaded with them to wed before his death. He'd died while they were still celebrating their wedding vows, and while his passing had saddened them, Maggie and Garrett both knew that Jason Intissar was in heaven.

Maggie nodded, but said nothing. Garrett continued, "Then winter set in, and we couldn't leave the valley."

"But that wasn't so bad," Maggie interrupted and leaned against Garrett. His arms went around her and pulled her close.

"I'm serious, Maggie. I want to take you on a honeymoon. Where would you like to go?"

"But Garrett, you, yourself, said that we're coming up on one of the busiest times for the ranch. The birthings and brandings, fence mendings, herds to be moved. . . ." Garrett put his finger on Maggie's lips.

"Hush," he said tenderly. "I can trust Mack to hire as many men as he needs. I'll send him to Springer to get the men he requires, but I am taking you away. Just you and me."

"All right," Maggie said, pushing away from Garrett's chest. "Where shall we go?"

"How do you feel about camping outdoors for several weeks? The place is really special, nothing like you've ever seen before." Maggie could hear the excitement in Garrett's voice.

"Sounds wonderful. When do we leave?" she answered enthusiastically.

"How about the end of the week?" Garrett questioned.

"That soon? Do you really think we could?" Maggie was starting to feel the excitement.

"I don't know why not. I'll talk to Mack when we get back to the ranch. In the meantime, Mrs. Lucas, come here and let me kiss you again." Maggie laughed and fell eagerly into her husband's arms. How good God was to her; how very good.

A shadowy veil lowered over the happiness in Maggie's heart. Lillie Johnston Philips, her best friend, was mourning the loss of her husband and baby. It seemed heartless to be this happy. Lillie was hundreds of miles away in Topeka, and Maggie was here with her brand new marriage.

Garrett sensed the change in Maggie's mood. "What is it?"

"I was just thinking about Lillie."

"You mustn't worry, Maggie," Garrett said sympathetically.

"I know, but I'd feel better if I could talk with her," Maggie said solemnly.

"You've done all you can, Maggie. You've extended our hospitality and told her that she'd be welcome to come and stay with us as long as she wants. There's nothing more to be done. Now I want you to stop worrying and start planning for our trip," Garrett said firmly but with a smile. Maggie nodded, knowing that he was right.

At the end of the week, Maggie happily joined Garrett in the corral. She mounted her horse and followed her husband west across the valley of Pinon Canyon Ranch. It was Garrett's plan to spend the night at the Pueblo Mission that Maggie's father had financed for Pastor David and Jenny Monroe.

They covered the twelve miles in a slow, deliberate manner, and Maggie enjoyed the crisp mountain air, despite the cool temperatures. The world was waking up from a long, silent sleep. Brilliant green shoots of range grass covered their way, as well as the regional spring flowers, Indian paintbrush, and gilia. Maggie breathed in deeply as if in doing so she could absorb all the sights and sounds of the land.

As they approached the two-story, adobe mission, Maggie's excitement increased. She hadn't seen Jenny Monroe since Christmas, and because Jenny was the only English-speaking woman in the area close to Maggie's age, Maggie missed her company.

Jenny and David came out into the yard to greet their friends. Behind Jenny and David trailed several shy, brown-skinned, Pueblo orphans.

"Garrett! Maggie!" Jenny was calling. "I didn't dare allow myself to get too excited until I actually saw you. Come on in and relax."

David waved from his wife's side. "Good to see you both," he added to Jenny's greeting.

That evening, Maggie worked with Jenny in the kitchen, while Garrett and David saw to the livestock.

"It's so good to have this time with you, Jenny," Maggie began.

"I know exactly what you mean," Jenny Monroe said with a sigh. "I was telling David not long after we received your letter about Lillie's accident that I wished I could be with you to offer any comfort I could. How is Lillie doing?"

Maggie's countenance changed, and her eyes betrayed the pain in her heart. "I wish I knew. Lillie hasn't written since her dismissal from the hospital. Her mother sent me two letters to keep me informed. She told me Lillie was grief stricken and not at all herself."

"That's a pity. It must be hard to lose a husband at such a young age. That's one grief I never hope to know about," Jenny said compassionately.

"Me either," Maggie said thoughtfully. "Nor the grief of losing a child."

Jenny grimaced.

"What is it, Jenny? Did I say something wrong?" Maggie questioned.

Jenny shook her head, but Maggie saw sadness in her eyes. Maggie stilled Jenny's bustlings with a hand upon her arm. "What is it Jenny?"

"I'm sorry, Maggie." Jenny wiped her hands on her

apron. "I guess Lillie's grief is one I can relate to after all. Come with me." Jenny walked out the kitchen door. Maggie followed obediently, until they'd walked well past the vegetable garden and several yards behind the house.

Jenny stopped before three, roughly hewn crosses. "My children," Jenny said in a soft, reflective manner. "They were too weak to live," she added.

Maggie felt a tightening in her chest. "Oh, Jenny," she said, near to tears. It was hard to imagine waiting and hoping for a baby, only to lose it.

Jenny touched Maggie's sleeve. "Don't be sad Maggie. I've mourned enough for both of us. They're with God. I know that much and comfort myself in the thought. Besides," she said, taking Maggie's hand in her own, "God's given me the orphaned Indian children."

Maggie fell silent for a few moments. She thought of the three small graves that held the earthly remains of Jenny's children. Her heart went out to her friend.

When Maggie finally spoke, there was fear as well as sadness in her voice. "I don't think I could bear it."

Jenny smiled. She, too, had thought herself unable to deal with the painful loss.

"God knows what we can and can't bear, Maggie. I don't have any answers for the whys, but I do know He is good to stand beside His own. Your Lillie must find comfort in that, too."

Maggie shook her head. "No, God is not a comfort to Lillie. She believes Him responsible for taking away her family. She is at war with God in a worse way than I was. Her mother wrote me to say that Lillie won't even tolerate going to church with the family. She stays in her room, secluded from the rest of the world."

"Poor thing," Jenny murmured "We must pray for her, Maggie. Remember, 'Where two or more are gathered in my name.' " Jenny Monroe's conviction in God's power was strong. "He will change Lillie's heart, Maggie, but we must continue to pray for her."

"If I hadn't gone through my own transformation with God, I would have thought it impossible to change Lillie's mind. Now, however," Maggie said with a new hope, "I know what God is capable of. I've seen firsthand how He can change a life. I want so much for Lillie to come to know God and to love Him as much as I do."

"Then have faith, Maggie. Have faith and let God do the rest. He doesn't always work as fast as we'd like Him to, but He's always got things under control. Even in this," Jenny said sweeping her hand past the three graves, "He was in control. I don't believe God killed my children, but I believe He allowed their passing. From it He has added blessings to me in mercy and compassion that I might never have learned otherwise."

"I hope one day that you'll get to meet, Lillie. I know that you'd be able to help her deal with her grief," Maggie said thoughtfully.

" I can do all things through Christ which strengtheneth me," Jenny quoted from Philippians. "It's never us, Maggie, but Christ in us. He is the One who gets us through, and He's the One who will see Lillie through."

Seeing the last slivers of pale lemon sun slip behind the snow-crested mountain peak, Jenny remembered her supper on the stove. "Oh my, we best get back to the kitchen, or there won't be anything but burnt roast for supper."

David and Garrett walked toward the house, the aroma

of supper heavy in the air. "Have you heard from him lately?" David questioned Garrett.

"I presume you mean your brother," Garrett replied as he stopped at the well to wash his hands and face. "The answer's no. I haven't heard from Daniel in months."

"I wish he would put the past behind him and come home," David said with a sadness that touched Garrett's heart. He, too, wished that his good friend would come back to the territory.

"We have to have hope, David," Garrett said as he put his hand on David's back.

"Yes, hope and faith in God to bring back the prodigal son," David sighed.

"Don't worry," Garrett reminded him, "God has worked with more stubborn people than your brother."

"I suppose you're right."

"I know I am. I was one of those more stubborn people." At Garrett's words, both men laughed, but the sadness was still shared between them. It was hard to wait for the lost to come home.

Springer, New Mexico, had proved to be anything but what Lillie had anticipated. She had envisioned leaving the train to find herself safely upon Lucas soil. When she learned that the ranch was several days' ride west, she fell into despair and disappointment.

She'd left word around town that she needed a ride to Pinon Canyon Ranch, but so far there had been no takers. Letting out a heavy sigh, Lillie threw herself across the iron-framed bed.

"What am I to do if nobody comes for me?" she questioned to the air.

When a knock sounded on her door, Lillie jumped from the bed. "Yes, who is it?" she called.

"It's your landlady." The hotel keeper's wife insisted on calling herself that. Lillie immediately unlocked and opened the door.

"What can I do for you?" Lillie questioned suspiciously.

"There's somebody in the lobby who wants to see you. A cowboy from the Pinon Canyon Ranch. You wanna see him or not?" The rotund woman moved from foot to foot as if nervously pacing in place.

"Of course I'll see him. Tell him I'll be right down," Lillie ordered and then saw the look of stubborn pride on the other woman's face. "Please," she added thinking it better to pacify her landlady. The woman nodded and disappeared down the hallway.

Lillie returned to her room and checked her hair and dress. She had chosen a simple calico print of dark blues and browns that she'd recently purchased in Springer. She grimaced as she thought of the reason for the new purchase. Her own clothes were growing tight again. Lillie pulled a dark brown shawl around her shoulders and went downstairs to greet her visitor.

"I'm Lillie," she said as she walked into the lobby. Mack Reynolds stood up and extended his hand.

"I'm Mack. Mack Reynolds," he added his last name as if to give his cowboy image more credibility. He could see this city woman was eyeing him warily. "I know you don't know me, but I'm Maggie and Garrett's foreman."

"I see," Lillie answered as if contemplating the job. "And you and Maggie are friends?"

"We sure are. I have the highest regards for Maggie Lucas."

"Well," Lillie said with a bit of hesitation in her voice, "I suppose I have no choice but to trust you."

Mack gave another broad smile. "You won't be sorry. I suppose you're wondering how I knew about you coming here."

"Well, no, not really. I did post a letter to the ranch a couple of days ago. I presumed you had received my note."

Mack laughed heartily. "I imagine that your letter is in one of the packs of mail I have on my wagon to take back with me to the ranch. We don't get our mail too regularly. Although they are hoping to put a post office in Bandelero one of these days."

"Bandelero?"

"That's right. We're in the process of creating a new town. It's really on Lucas land, but Maggie and Garrett decided it would be in everybody's best interest to develop a trading post closer to home. Bandelero is expanding pretty quicklike, and now we're waiting for the post office to be approved."

"I see," Lillie replied, not completely sure that she did see at all. It was going to be difficult to adjust her thinking to the less-civilized world that she'd thrown herself into. "Then how did you know that I would be arriving in Springer?" Lillie finally questioned.

"Your mother sent a letter. The trouble is, Maggie and Garrett have gone away on a little trip. I expect them back in a few days, but when I saw your mother's letter marked *urgent*, I took the liberty of checking it out. She mentioned when you'd be arriving, and since I had to come to Springer to hire men for the roundup, I figured I could pick you up as well."

"How considerate of you," Lillie replied, meaning

every word. She was thankful that her mother had had the sense to send a letter to Maggie.

"I have only one problem, Mrs. Philips." Mack paused for a moment, noticing Lillie's frown. "Would you rather I call you Lillie?"

"I. . .well. . . ," Lillie stammered before answering. "Yes. I do prefer it. Sometimes hearing myself called by my married name serves to be a painful reminder of what I've lost." She had no desire to explain her train transformation.

"I understand," Mack replied seriously. "The problem is that we're set to leave this afternoon. Can you be ready that quickly?"

Lillie gave a surprising laugh. "I was ready to leave here the day I arrived. I'll have my things waiting in the lobby whenever you need me to."

Mack smiled. "Great. I'll be back for you in two hours."

"I shall look forward to it," Lillie acknowledged.

six

The trip to Pinon Canyon was rough, but uneventful. Lillie had never camped outdoors and found it frightening, but without a hotel or boarding house along the many miles of mountain terrain, there was nothing else to do. After nearly a week of being jostled back and forth, they arrived at Maggie and Garrett's ranch.

"It's beautiful!" Lillie exclaimed. "I had no idea. Maggie told me about the ranch and she'd said that it was breathtaking, but her letters didn't do it justice."

Mack agreed. "I could never call any place else home."

"I can understand why," Lillie replied.

As they approached the adobe ranch house, Mack began to explain a few things about the house. "You'll be the only woman in the house until Maggie comes home. Maria, that was our cook, took off to spend some time with her family. Besides, Maggie's come to enjoy caring for the house herself."

"Really?" Lillie questioned. She couldn't imagine enjoying the tasks and chores that a large house would demand. The thought of learning to cook had never interested Lillie.

"Why sure," Mack said with a lopsided grin. "She's a pretty fair cook, too." It was almost as if he'd read Lillie's mind. "Of course," Mack went on, "it wasn't always so. Maria had to throw out a few batches while teaching her how to make tortillas."

"Tortillas?" Lillie questioned, wondering at the strange sounding word.

"It's what we use a lot in place of bread. Course, Maggie makes good bread, as well. But tortillas are nice for a change. They're round like a dish and thin. You can make 'em out of flour or corn, and then you fry 'em up and eat 'em."

"Sounds interesting," Lillie admitted. She was beginning to realize that she was quite hungry, and the talk of food wasn't helping one bit.

"I might add," Mack continued, "that we have a friend of Garrett's staying with us. He just arrived the other day." Mack reined back on the horses and brought the wagon to a stop. "I don't suppose he'll be any bother to you. I'll just set you up in Maggie's old room, and he'll be clear down the other end of the hall. You probably won't even see much of him."

"I really don't mind, Mack," Lillie answered honestly. "I think I've been alone too long, anyway. Having you to talk to has opened my eyes to that, not to mention all the things I've learned about New Mexico."

"I'm glad," Mack said as he threw the reins to another cowboy. "Let me help you down, and I'll get you settled inside."

Lillie allowed Mack to usher her into Maggie's home. It seemed strange that Lillie would learn all about it from a ranch hand rather than from Maggie. She listened half-heartedly to Mack explain where she could find things she might need. Mack was just explaining that she should feel free to scout out the kitchen, when a familiar voice sounded behind them.

"Garrett? Is that you?"

Lillie whirled around to find herself face to face with Daniel Monroe. "You!" she exclaimed in complete surprise.

Daniel raised a mocking eyebrow, enjoying Lillie's discomfort before answering simply, "Me."

Lillie felt the color rise to her cheeks as Mack explained that he was just showing Lillie to the kitchen.

"Well that's one place I'm certain Lillie will want to know the whereabouts of," Daniel said sarcastically.

"You are a complete beast," Lillie said, stomping her foot. "Why don't you leave me alone and mind your own business?"

Mack was bewildered by the entire encounter. "I take it you two know each other?" he questioned.

"Why, yes. Lillie and I met on the train, Mack. If I'd realized she was coming to Pinon Canyon, I'd have offered her a ride on the back of my horse," Daniel remarked. The glint in his eye and the ever-so-mocking tone to his voice caused Lillie to speak.

"But then that would have placed too much weight on the poor animal." She thought she was delivering his comeuppance, but Daniel, true to form, had the final word.

"Yes, you're right, Lillie. I don't think poor old Scout would have been able to endure both the extra weight and the mountain roads." With that, Daniel started to move down the hallway, chuckling to himself as he did. "I fix a superb supper, Lillie. I do hope you'll join me, as we'll be the only ones here."

"I'd rather starve," Lillie yelled after him. Her remark only invoked more laughter from Daniel, and a deeply puzzled expression on the face of Mack.

"I am sorry, Mack. Dr. Monroe isn't very pleasant

company for me. I would go elsewhere if I could, but since there's no where else to go, I will simply stay in my room as much as possible." Mack nodded his head.

"Now," Lillie continued, "I believe you were going to show me to my room."

"Sure thing, Lillie," Mack said and led Lillie down the hall.

When the last hint of sunlight faded behind the mountain peaks, Lillie lit the lamp in her room and began to pace the floor. She was starving, yet hadn't she told Daniel she'd rather do that than endure his company?

There wasn't a moment that she didn't remember Daniel's hurtful remarks. Why did he have to goad her so? She'd been rude to him; that much was true. But had she truly earned the disrespect and cruelty that he seemed intent on giving?

Lillie tried to busy herself by arranging her clothes in the wardrobe and cleaning up from the long, dusty trip. She washed her hair for the first time since she'd cut it and found it a much simpler task. As her hair dried, Lillie noticed the slightest wave to it's baby fine texture. She decided to leave it down, enjoying the feel of it as it bounced against her shoulders. She then donned a white shirtwaist and dark burgundy skirt and sat down to work at her cross-stitch.

By nine o'clock, Lillie could no longer stand the hunger pains. She'd done everything possible to ignore them, but it was useless. A person was entitled to eat three meals a day; even Dr. Daniel Monroe would have to agree with that.

Lillie cautiously opened her bedroom door and peeked

down the hall. Hadn't Mack told her that Daniel's room was at the end of the hall? Seeing no one about, Lillie gingerly stepped into the hallway and walked silently to the kitchen.

A lamp burned on the small kitchen table, and Lillie picked it up and went to the stove. Someone had left a covered dish on the back edge, and Lillie lifted the towel to find a wonderful dinner. A thick slice of ham made Lillie's mouth water and there was a good-sized portion of fried potatoes as well.

"I saved it for you," Daniel's voice called from the doorway.

"I thought you'd gone to bed," Lillie replied. She was trying hard to keep her feelings in check.

"No," Daniel shrugged, "I was waiting to see how long it took you to come out here for something to eat."

"Why do you find such pleasure in hurting me?" Lillie questioned him against her will. "I hardly see what I've done to deserve such severity."

Daniel's expression softened a bit. He hadn't intended to hurt her feelings. It just didn't seem right for such a beautiful woman to destroy herself by overeating.

"I'm sorry, Lillie," Daniel offered. "I hadn't intended on hurting your feelings. It just grieves me to see a woman with your kind of looks deprive herself of a healthy body."

Lillie couldn't begin to tell Daniel how much it grieved her to be in the shape she was, but it was like a snowball rolling downhill, picking up more snow as it went. Once the weight started coming on, she ate even more.

"I don't see where that gives you the right to insult me. Suggestions are one thing. They tend to be more compassionate and helpful. Insults just make me mad," Lillie answered honestly.

"I've a feeling that you've had plenty of pity and compassion. That's the bad thing about mourning. You can very easily be pitied and sympathized into a depressive stupor. Maybe if someone had the nerve to stand up to you, like I'm doing, you'd see the situation for what it is and take better care of yourself."

Lillie's rage returned. She'd tried very hard to deal with Daniel's words as evenly and calmly as possible, but he wasn't making it at all easy. "I don't know why you've chosen to appoint yourself my keeper, but I don't need your help, so please leave me alone."

"Yes, I can see that you're doing a great job," Daniel remarked sarcastically.

Lillie could take no more. Reaching down to the stove beside her, she picked up the cast iron skillet and in blind fury plunged at Daniel.

The move took Daniel by surprise, but not so much that he didn't have a good time with the furious woman before him. He took off running and laughing which only caused Lillie to become more incensed.

Mindless to what she was doing, Lillie's only desire was to vent her frustration. Months of anger at herself and everyone else came pouring out as she chased Daniel from room to room. His laughter egged her on, and his sarcastic barbs gave her added energy.

With the skillet raised high above her head, Lillie picked up her skirts and ran in earnest, thinking only of planting the iron pan fully against Daniel's skull.

Just as Daniel ran past the front entry door, Maggie and Garrett Lucas returned from their honeymoon.

"Daniel?" Garrett said in amazement at the laughing

man who was dodging blows from a plump, blond woman.

"Lillie?" Maggie breathed and looked up to find Garrett's questioning eyes looking down at her.

"Lillie?" Garrett questioned Maggie.

Maggie nodded her head in acknowledgement while Lillie continued to strike out at Daniel. Regaining her wits from the shock of seeing Lillie, Maggie called out to her.

"Lillie! Lillie! Stop this at once!"

Daniel was laughing so hard that it became infectious, and Garrett started to snicker, too.

"Don't you dare," Maggie said turning a stern look on her husband. Garrett only laughed harder.

"Lillie, did you hear me?" Maggie called out, taking a step forward.

"Please, ma'am," Daniel called between his hysterical laughter, "don't stop her. It's the most exercise she's had in months."

At this, Lillie threw the skillet. Daniel easily dodged the missile, but then Lillie threw herself at him as well. She was beating his chest and trying to bite his hand as he took hold of her arms.

"No fair biting, Lillie, unless I get to bite back," Daniel said as he sobered somewhat.

Garrett was still laughing, and Maggie stood with her hands on her hips. "Will somebody tell me what's going on here? This is my house you're fighting in. And will you stop laughing!" Maggie said as she took hold of her husband's shoulders and gave him a light shaking.

Garrett lifted her high in the air and smiled. "I think you were more manageable on the trail. Maybe we should go back to the mountains."

Maggie started to kick her booted feet in protest. "Put

me down, Garrett. Lillie needs me."

Garrett glanced past his wife to where Daniel had Lillie pinned against his chest and laughed. "I don't think Lillie knows what she's up against. I've wrestled with Daniel Monroe before," he said as he put Maggie back on the ground, "and he's a hard man to beat."

Maggie rolled her eyes. "A lot of help you are!" She turned to go to Lillie, but Garrett held her fast. "I think we'd better let them work this out themselves."

"Maggie, don't you leave me here with this monster!" Lillie called out, as Garrett began dragging Maggie down the hallway.

"Garrett, stop! She needs me," Maggie protested, but to no avail.

Lillie gave up on Maggie as her friend disappeared behind the dining room door. She tried to free herself, but became acutely aware of the man restraining her.

Daniel had wrapped one arm around Lillie's waist and the other across her shoulders. She tried to kick him, but her feet became tangled in her skirts and nearly sent them both onto the floor.

"If you would kindly stop fighting me, I'll let you go," Daniel whispered against Lillie's ear. He could smell the sweetness of her hair and, despite her added weight, Daniel liked the feel of Lillie in his arms.

The revelation came to him like a flash of lightning, and he suddenly released his grip. Lillie bolted from his arms and ran with all her might to her bedroom. She was ashamed to find herself crying by the time she reached the door and was barely aware that Daniel had followed her and was now pounding on her locked door.

She threw herself across the bed and cried. The pain in

her throat seemed to constrict normal breathing, and Lillie struggled to catch her breath. She was hysterical, wheezing and gasping. She'd never cried this hard, not even after the doctor had told her Jason was dead.

Lillie began to feel lightheaded and struggled to sit up in order to get her breath. It didn't help. The more shallowly and rapidly she breathed, the worse she felt. Just then the door flew open and Daniel was at her side.

"Shhh," he whispered as he held her. "Just take deep breaths." Lillie's strained breathing slowed, though the tears still fell silently.

"Look, Lillie, I'm sorry. I'll stop with the remarks about your weight. Truce?" Daniel asked earnestly. He hated causing her such pain. What had started out as good-natured teasing had turned quite ugly, and he regretted that he was responsible.

Lillie looked up into Daniel's eyes. They were steely blue and looked as if they could see into her soul. "All right," she said and swallowed hard. "Truce."

"You rest now, and I'll go get Maggie," Daniel said as he got up to leave. Lillie nodded and watched him walk out the door.

Outside, Daniel sighed and leaned back against the cool stone wall. He couldn't get one thought out of his mind: the thought of Lillie in his arms. How good it had felt to touch another human being, especially one as beautiful as Lillie. And she was beautiful, Daniel knew. Despite the added weight and her anger, Lillie was very nearly charming him out of his memories.

Daniel felt a tremor of excitement course through his blood. It both grieved him and thrilled him. He knew that forever mourning his Katie's death would never bring her back.

But now, another image filled his mind. Lillie. The scent of her hair and the softness of its fine texture against his face. Desperate to shake the memory, he went in search of Maggie.

seven

Maggie sat cooling her heels in the dining room while
Garrett tried to ease her worries.

"Look, Maggie, I know Daniel. We can trust him to
work out whatever problem he and Lillie are having.
She'll be just fine with him," Garrett said as he rubbed his
wife's shoulders. Maggie was nervously twisting a piece
of the fine linen tablecloth.

"I hope so," Maggie answered. She was still in shock
from finding Lillie at the ranch. "I wish she'd told me that
she was coming. I begged her for months to come stay with
us, but I never expected her to show up without any word."

Garrett reached down and pulled Maggie into his arms.
"Don't worry, my beloved," he said and placed a light kiss
on her forehead.

"I hate to interrupt," a voice called from the doorway,
"but Lillie wants to see you." It was Daniel.

Maggie looked up curiously at the tall, sandy-haired
man. He seemed harmless enough. "What in the world was
all that about?" Maggie questioned.

"Maybe it would be better for Lillie to explain. She's
waiting in her room," Daniel answered. "In the meantime," he continued, "I'm Dr. Daniel Monroe, but I hope
you'll call me Daniel." He extended his hand to Maggie
and smiled broadly.

Maggie turned to take his hand while Garrett stood with
his arm firmly fixed around her waist. "I'm Maggie,

66

Garrett's wife."

Daniel nodded. "I would've known you without the introduction. Garrett used to write me long letters extolling all your virtues."

Maggie laughed as she cast a sidelong glance at her husband. "Those letters couldn't have been all that long."

"On the contrary," Daniel began, but Garrett quickly interrupted.

"I think you'd better go to Lillie," Garrett said as he nudged Maggie in the direction of the door. "As for you," he said taking Daniel by the arm, "we have quite a bit to catch up on."

"Very well," Daniel said with a shrug of his shoulders and a smile for Maggie. "I can always tell her about it later."

Maggie laughed at the look of discomfort on her husband's face. "I shall look forward to it, Daniel. I hope you'll be staying with us for a while." With that, Maggie took off in search of Lillie.

Making her way down the hallway, Maggie was pleased to see that Mack had put Lillie in her old room. Maggie rather missed the quaintness of the bedroom her father had designed for her.

Lillie was sitting on the edge of the bed when Maggie walked into the room. "Maggie!" she exclaimed as she rushed into her friend's arms.

"I can't believe you're really here, Lillie. Why didn't you write and tell me?"

"I'm sorry, Maggie. It was very rude of me to arrive unannounced. Mother suggested the change of scenery, and she knew how dearly I missed you. Please forgive me for not announcing myself first," Lillie said as she pulled away from Maggie's embrace.

Maggie took a good look at her friend, and the scrutiny, even from her dear friend, made Lillie uncomfortable. "Hard to believe isn't it?" Lillie sighed the question. "This time last year I was enjoying engagement parties, and you and I were planning my wedding. Now this," she said with a sweep of her arm across her body.

Maggie was grateful that Lillie had made reference to the past. She had struggled to think of a way to tell Lillie how sorry she was for Jason's death. "Lillie, I'm so sorry about Jason and the baby. I wish there were words to express my pain for you. Are you able to talk about it?"

Lillie shook her head. "Not really. I vowed to put that part of my life behind me."

"Is that wise?" Maggie questioned.

"I don't know, Maggie. All I know is that I very nearly threw myself off the train on the way down here. I don't want to feel like that again, and if that means forgetting about Jason and the baby, then that's what I have to do."

"Lillie, why don't we go out into the courtyard," Maggie suggested. "We can sit and have a good long talk, and I'll get us some refreshments." Then noticing the lateness of the hour for the first time, Maggie added, "Unless of course you're too tired. We could always wait and talk tomorrow."

"No," Lillie replied, feeling a need to talk. "I'd like to spend some time with you. I've missed our long talks."

"Me, too," Maggie said with a beckoning arm. "Come on. I'll get us something to eat and have Garrett light the courtyard lanterns."

"All right. Just don't let Daniel see that you're feeding me. He thinks I should starve rather than gain more weight," Lillie commented snidely as she followed Maggie into the hallway.

Later when they were seated in the cobblestone court-yard, Maggie asked Lillie to elaborate on her argument with Daniel. "Was it the issue of eating that caused the fight I witnessed?" Maggie questioned as she poured hot coffee for Lillie and herself.

"That and his rudeness," Lillie answered. "I'd simply had all I could take of Dr. Monroe's sarcasm." She reached down to put a liberal amount of sugar and cream in her coffee.

"Why don't you tell me about it," Maggie suggested. "How did you and Daniel meet?"

Lillie grimaced at the memory of the pregnant woman. She struggled to put the ghastly moment into words. "Daniel needed my train car to deliver a baby," Lillie began. "I refused when the conductor asked me. Maggie, I just couldn't handle the idea of a woman delivering a baby before my eyes; especially when my own baby would have been due about the same time."

"Of course you couldn't," Maggie sympathized.

"Daniel wouldn't take no for an answer and knocked down my door." Lillie reached out and took one of the thick slices of bread that Maggie offered. "It was a nightmare, Maggie. All of it," Lillie said, realizing that she meant the accident as much as anything. "Jason had started to change," Lillie continued. "I was quite harsh with him about the changes, but we managed to make up before the accident."

"I'm certain that no matter what the problems between you and Jason, he knew you loved him. You mustn't be so hard on yourself, Lillie."

Lillie put down her empty cup and shifted her weight uncomfortably. "After the accident, I started eating and eating. I wanted so much to numb my mind to the pain. I wanted to forget my grief, and. . . ." Lillie's words fell away.

"And?" Maggie encouraged her to continue.

"And I didn't want to look anything like the woman Jason loved. I didn't want to be any part of that woman, that life." Lillie got up and paced back and forth.

"Is that why you cut your hair, Lillie?"

"Yes, although I must say, that's the only change I don't mind," Lillie admitted. She was desperate to purge herself of the emotions buried within. "Maggie, I hate myself. I hate looking this way. I hate feeling this way. I get up in the morning, hoping against hope that it's all been nothing more than a bad dream, but of course it's quite real. I just can't bear it at times. Will the pain ever go away?"

Maggie smiled sadly. "I think so. I know I still miss my father, but the pain isn't near what it was a month ago or two months before that. It isn't that I don't love him as much as I did before he died, it just doesn't hurt as much now. Of course, my loss was much different than yours. You lost a husband and a child," Maggie said noticing Lillie's frown. "I think the sooner you face up to that loss and go on, the better you'll be."

"I'm trying, Maggie. I wanted to change my appearance, but not like this," Lillie said, near to tears. "Daniel never misses an opportunity to make some comment about it. That's why I was so angry. I came out to get some supper, and he was there to make fun of me."

Maggie frowned. "How cruel. I shall have to speak to our Dr. Monroe about his manners."

"You don't need to, Maggie. We have a truce of sorts. At least that's what he promised."

"So you will stay with us for a while, in spite of Daniel's presence?" Maggie questioned.

Lillie hadn't considered how long she'd stay with Maggie. There was nothing in Topeka to go back to and certainly no reason to concern herself with any kind of schedule. "I'll stay as long as you want me," Lillie said with a sad smile.

"Then you'll never go home," Maggie replied earnestly, "because I shall want you here always."

Days later, Maggie and Lillie had fallen into a routine of rising early to talk and bake. Maggie was teaching Lillie how to make bread, and Lillie was trying to work through her bitter emotions.

"Lillie," Maggie began one morning, "do you still enjoy riding?"

"I suppose I would, but with this additional weight, I'm not sure the horse would."

"Nonsense," Maggie rebuked matter-of-factly. "Garrett and Daniel outweigh you many times over, and they've been enjoying daily rides. I think we should spend some time outdoors. You'd be surprised what the fresh mountain air will do for you, and the exercise will make you feel alive again."

"I'm not certain that I want to feel alive," Lillie said as she kneaded a lump of dough. "I really don't have any reason to live."

"Lillie, you have many reasons to live," Maggie said as she placed her hand lightly on Lillie's arm. "Please don't give up."

Lillie sighed. "I came here in hopes of finding a place

to heal; even a way to heal. But Maggie I just don't feel good about anything. I'm numb."

"Lillie, God will see you through this. He can give you the answers you're looking for."

Lillie stiffened noticeably and moved away from her friend. "Don't talk to me about God, Maggie. I don't need religion, and I don't need God. I have plenty of money to buy what I need, and I can go anywhere in the world; so if you insist on preaching at me, I'll leave."

Maggie was stunned. Her mouth dropped open in surprise. Lillie's anger and bitterness toward God seemed so overwhelming. Maggie dared to force the issue. "Lillie, what is this all about?"

Lillie left the bread on the floured board and wiped her hands on the white apron that Maggie had lent her. "Jason got religion before he died. It was the reason we were fighting. I just know that God took Jason away from me, and the baby as well, because I was angry that Jason had become a Christian. Maggie, I want no part of a God that would do a thing like that."

"Lillie, God didn't kill Jason, and He certainly didn't kill your baby. Things often happen in life because of our disobedience or sinfulness, but I don't believe that God would take the life of your husband and child just to prove a point."

"Maggie, you never used to care what God thought. You were angry at Him yourself, and I never preached at you when you couldn't see a reason to believe in Him. I expect no less from you."

"But, Lillie," Maggie tried to reason. "You're miserable because of your loss. I'm trying to tell you that there is a way for you to see your husband and baby again."

Lillie reached out and in a flash of anger slapped Maggie across the face. "How dare you!"

Tears filled Maggie's eyes. This wasn't the Lillie with whom she'd spent years of companionship with. This wasn't the Lillie she'd longed to return home to see. Maggie stared at Lillie for a moment longer before answering. "I dare because it's true," she whispered.

Lillie's temper abated a bit. "I'm sorry, Maggie," she said without emotion. "Maybe I should pack my things and leave."

Maggie stepped forward, took hold of Lillie's shoulders, and forced her to look Maggie in the eye. "You can run if you like, Lillie. You can leave me and never allow me the pleasure of our friendship again. But you will never outrun God. Now I propose we settle our differences and enjoy a nice long visit, but that's only my desire. If it isn't yours, then I understand."

Tears formed in Lillie's eyes. She was grieved at the angry red welt that had formed on Maggie's cheek. "It's my desire, too, Maggie. I do want to stay. I can't abide the thought of losing your friendship, nor can I live with the idea of returning to Topeka. At least not yet."

"Good," Maggie said and gave Lillie's shoulders a squeeze. "Then I won't preach at you any more. However, I wish you would allow me to help you in another way."

Maggie noticed Lillie's eyes narrow slightly. When Lillie didn't make any move to disagree, Maggie continued.

"I know that you're miserable with yourself. I remember how much you prided yourself on your figure, and I want to help you lose the weight you've gained. I want to help you regain your health. Then, if and when you return to Topeka, you'll have no reason to be distressed with your physical state."

Lillie breathed a sigh of relief. "I'd be very happy to have your help, Maggie. I've really made a mess of myself, haven't I?"

Maggie laughed and dropped her hold on Lillie. "Not at all. Now what do you say we go for a ride? This bread has to rise anyway."

eight

Garrett was having every bit as much trouble with the stubborn Dr. Monroe as Maggie was having with Lillie. Daniel and Garrett had a past that went back several years, but even that long a friendship couldn't break down the strained wall that Daniel had erected.

"I'm glad you finally came back," Garrett said as he and Daniel settled down to breakfast.

Daniel didn't reply, and Maggie and Lillie walked into the room. "Garrett, Lillie and I are going riding," Maggie announced as she pulled on her riding gloves.

"Not without a kiss, you aren't," Garrett said, taking hold of Maggie's gloved hand.

"I wouldn't dream of it," Maggie said joyfully and bent down to receive her husband's kiss.

Maggie and Garrett missed the pained look on Lillie's face, but Daniel didn't. He struggled with the feeling of wanting to comfort her. She was standing close enough to touch, yet Daniel held fast, not wanting to cause her more heartache.

"Please be careful," Garrett said, breaking the spell Daniel found himself under.

"Of course we will," Maggie said and smiled. "I'm anxious to show Lillie the ranch, so don't worry about us. I've packed some dried fruit and cheese. Don't look for us until late."

Daniel lowered his face to keep from showing Lillie the

smile that brightened his face. Maggie had told him that Lillie had put herself in Maggie's care in order to lose weight. Daniel told himself that it was his doctor's observant eye, and not his interest in Lillie Philips, that caused him to believe she was well on her way to recovering her trim waistline.

Once Maggie and Lillie were out of the house, Garrett passed Daniel a platter with two large fried steaks on it. "One nice thing about ranch life is that the beef is no farther away than your back door."

"I must say your choice of breakfast food is different from my usual fare," Daniel replied and helped himself to one of the steaks.

"You work hard out here, and a hearty breakfast is always called for. Even Maggie eats a great deal more than she used to," Garrett laughed and passed Daniel a heaping bowl of scrambled eggs.

"She's definitely working wonders with Lillie," Daniel said, trying to sound nonchalant.

"You kind of like her, don't you?" Garrett questioned between bites.

"I'd rather not discuss it," Daniel answered, leaving Garrett to realize the subject was closed.

"Well then, maybe you'd be interested in knowing that David and Jenny have missed you. They'll be happy to see you. Have you let them know that you're here?"

"No and I don't intend to," Daniel said sternly. "I didn't come back to the territory to get a sermon, so I'd just as soon avoid my brother."

"But he really cares about you, Daniel. He was asking me a couple of weeks ago if I'd heard from you and how you were doing. You can't fault the man for caring about his only brother," Garrett reasoned.

Daniel dropped his fork to his plate. "My family business is just that, my business. I don't intend to be harassed by you or anyone else. I only returned because...," Daniel paused for a moment, "because, I can't get this place out of my mind. It's in my blood. I thought when Katie died that I'd never want to see this place again, but I was wrong. Images of the mountains, the smell of the Pinon pines, the way the air stays fresh and crisp well into the summer heat—I couldn't forget it." Daniel had a faraway look in his eyes. It had been over six years since he'd been in New Mexico, yet in many ways he'd never left at all.

"You know me better than to believe I'm sticking my nose in your affairs. I just thought you might care," Garrett replied completely annoyed with his friend.

"I do care, Garrett, but not the way you think I should. So maybe we'd better forget about it," Daniel said and continued to eat his meal in silence.

"Well, let's see. That's two subjects we can't discuss. Do you have a list of any others?" Garrett drawled sarcastically.

"Don't go getting on your high horse with me, Garrett. I've got some problems, we both know that. What I don't need is for you to pass judgment on me. I don't need to have to answer to you or anyone else."

"Not even God?"

"Especially not God," Daniel retorted. He was having difficulty keeping his anger in check.

"So what do you want to talk about?" Garrett inquired.

"Actually," Daniel began, "there is something I want to talk to you about."

"And what's that?" Garrett questioned curiously.

"I've been considering opening up an office in Bandelero," Daniel replied as he pushed the cleaned plate back and poured himself another cup of coffee.

"Dan, that's great news. We got word a month or so ago that our regular doctor was leaving the area. His wife can't abide the solitary life, and they're returning to St. Louis," Garrett said as he joined Daniel in a second cup of coffee.

"So you think folks would accept me into the community? Most of them don't know me from before," Daniel said with some reserve. "And, to be quite honest, after losing Katie, I've never had the same confidence in my abilities. I'm really not certain I'd be the asset that you seem to think I'd be."

"Nonsense," Garrett said trying to dispel Daniel's lack of self-confidence. "You have the schooling, the training, and the heart. I know you'd be welcomed with open arms."

"There's still the element of being a stranger to most of these people," Daniel argued.

"But you are David's brother, and around here that will count for a great deal. People hold your brother in high esteem," Garrett offered. He'd hoped that the words would make Daniel realize how beneficial David could be in helping him get established in Bandelero.

"No doubt they do," Daniel said sarcastically. "I don't need to concern David with my plans."

"He'll hear about them," Garrett replied.

"Hearing about them and being a part of them are two different things. I don't need his help," Daniel insisted, and Garrett realized they were once again at a critical impasse.

"All right, Daniel, we'll leave David out of this. What did you have in mind?" Garrett questioned as he pushed away from the table.

"I have some plans in my room. Why don't I get them, and we can discuss the matter in detail," Daniel offered.

Hours later, Daniel and Garrett were still pouring over Daniel's plans. "In time I hope to add onto this office space, and make it a small hospital."

"In time? Why wait?" Garrett asked as he studied the blueprints.

"Buildings cost money, and so do the supplies necessary to make a true hospital," Daniel replied. "I've only saved enough to build the office and examining room. I figured I could put a bed in the office and live there as well."

"What if I joined you as a partner?" Garrett questioned, and Daniel's face broke into a smile.

"Are you serious?" Daniel questioned enthusiastically. Suddenly he could see all his dreams coming true.

"I wouldn't have said it if I weren't serious," Garrett replied. "I have plenty of money. What I didn't inherit from my own folks, Maggie and I inherited from her father. Then there's the amount I've saved up over the last few years and the profits from the ranch. I'm more than capable of helping you achieve your goals and benefiting the community at the same time. So what do you say? Partners?"

Daniel slapped his hand into Garrett's outstretched one. "Partners," he said with gladness.

The moment of joy was dispelled as Maggie came bursting through the door with David Monroe close behind.

"Look who I found!" Maggie exclaimed. "Daniel, it's your brother, and he didn't know you were here."

David's eager face revealed his desire to reach out to his

brother. Daniel, however, fixed a scowl to his face, and his
steel blue eyes darkened in anger.

Garrett pulled Maggie aside. "Where's Lillie?" he
asked.

"She offered to take the horses to the barn. Why?"
Maggie questioned, as she realized the tension between
Daniel and David. "What's wrong, Garrett?"

"Come on, let's make sure Lillie doesn't need our help."

Daniel refused to speak. He was too angry. If he'd never
had to deal with David again, it would have been too soon.

"Dan, I wondered if I'd ever see you again," David said
as he stepped forward to embrace his brother.

"You've seen me," Daniel said in a stilted voice. "Now,
if you'll excuse me. . . ."

"Please stay, Daniel. Can't we talk?" David was beg-
ging, he knew, but it was important to him.

"No," Daniel said as he turned to leave the room. "We
can't."

Harbored back in his room, Daniel sat down in a red
leather chair. He was fuming at being forced to meet David
head-on. It wasn't Maggie's fault, he realized, but she had
brought him back to the house. Garrett must never have
explained his differences with David. It would be like
Garrett to keep things to himself, but in this case, Daniel
wished that Garrett had told Maggie of his estrangement
from his brother.

Unable to sit still, Daniel began to pace the room. It was
a large room with whitewashed adobe walls and a dome-
shaped wood stove in one corner. There was a massive
four-poster bed with several layers of richly woven Indian
blankets to ward off the cold of night, and a large oak
wardrobe, which held all of Daniel's worldly belongings.

The money he'd managed to save for the office he hoped to build was sitting in his valise.

Daniel looked around the room and felt alien to everything in it. There weren't any memories here, and outside of the Indian pottery and blankets to remind him of the New Mexico home he'd once shared with David, there was nothing here that spoke of home.

Daniel pounded his fists against the adobe wall until they were scuffed and bleeding. Why did he have to feel this anger? Why did the rage continue? Wasn't six years of torment enough?

Having spent his energy at the wall, Daniel sat back down in the leather chair. Leaning over the desk, he put his face in his hands. "Oh, Katie," he whispered aloud, "how ashamed you must be of me."

Daniel thought of the petite young woman he'd married so many years ago. The delicate, young blond had lied to him and to David about her age, so it wasn't until after they were married that Daniel learned that his wife was only sixteen years old. In many ways, Katie Monroe had been wise beyond her years.

She had been suited to Daniel, who was finishing up his residency in a major Kansas City hospital, and before Daniel had realized what had happen, he had proposed and they were married. Daniel smiled when he remembered Katie's willingness to learn new things; she had wanted to act as his nurse and had offered to go to school for training. Daniel couldn't have asked for more in a wife.

Then they'd found themselves in the uncivilized West, and Katie was pregnant. Neither of them felt any concern because Daniel was, after all, a doctor. It wasn't important that they be in a big town or organized community. They had each other and that was enough. At least it was supposed to have been.

Daniel sighed. Things had been so different then. He'd shared David's faith in God, believed the words of the Bible that God's love was everlasting and that His mercies were new each day. That had been before Katie died.

The baby had refused to be born, and David and Jenny had come to offer support and prayers. Daniel labored with his young wife, struggling to help her deliver their baby, but nothing worked. Daniel begged David to plead with God for Katie's life, as well as the life of their unborn child. David had agree to pray, but for God's will, not for Daniel's dictated request.

Katie had died, and it was God's will. Daniel decided then and there to turn his face from God and from his brother. How could he accept that the will of a merciful God had been to claim the life of his wife and child? Why would a loving God leave him alone and take the only woman he would ever care about?

Lillie's face came to mind, and Daniel grimaced. Guilt-ridden, he pressed his hands against the sides of his head. Was it possible that he cared more about Lillie than he was willing to admit? In many ways, Lillie and he shared a common bond, but what was the purpose of that bond?

So many questions surged through his mind. Maybe returning to New Mexico had been the wrong thing. If he hadn't come, he would never have met Lillie.

For a moment, Daniel allowed the picture of Lillie to permeate his thoughts. She was a good woman, and she was working so hard to improve herself and get back into the routine of living. She deserved better than what he could give her. She was used to the fine life and the big city.

Surely she would never be interested in considering him as a lifelong companion.

Where had that come from? Daniel wondered. One minute he was thinking about his beloved Katie, and the next minute it was Lillie.

Tormented by the vision of both women, Daniel was further disturbed by the memory of David's face. David had come with such hope and enthusiasm. He had come to bury the past and embrace the future with his older brother, and Daniel had sent him away empty handed.

The look on David's face haunted Daniel. How could he have caused his own brother such pain? The truth be told, he'd wanted to hug David the minute he'd walked into the room. He'd missed his little brother and the closeness they'd shared for so many years.

Daniel tried to ignore the hurt he felt inside. There was no way that he could deal with David. To put aside his differences with David meant coming to terms with God, and that was something that Daniel Monroe was not inclined to do.

nine

September 1879 was a glorious and bountiful time of harvest. The Pueblo Indians had come to Pinon Canyon to trade agricultural products and sheep for beef and horses. Garrett was happy to oblige them as the small garden that Maggie and Lillie had cared for throughout the summer wasn't large enough to feed the ranch through the winter months.

Grain sacks provided by the ranch were filled with a variety of corn. Then the Indians brought in several baskets of apples, squash, and pumpkins. Garrett praised the Indians for their wealth of crops. More than one visitor credited the bounty to the Blue Corn Clan and their summer corn dance, as well as to the Cloud People who were always credited for good corn crops. Garrett didn't contradict them but added a simple statement: "God has been very good to us, hasn't He!"

Lillie got her first lessons in canning from Maggie and Maria, Maggie's cook. She seemed to take to the laborious task in a way that surprised even Maggie. Standing over the outdoor caldron one afternoon, Lillie was amazed to discover that she was actually enjoying herself.

Lillie knew that her happiness was multifaceted. Glancing down at her trim and tiny waist, she wanted to pinch herself to make certain she wasn't dreaming. The weight loss was real, however, and Lillie felt as if a burden of more than flesh had been lifted.

When Daniel and Garrett rode into the yard, Maggie immediately handed her canning duties over to Maria and went to seek out the men. She noticed how Lillie watched Daniel, and wondered if she was developing feelings for the older man.

Garrett was already busy with one of the ranch hands, but Maggie didn't mind. She wanted to talk to Daniel. Making her way into the barn, she found the doctor caring for his horse.

"Daniel, I wonder if you have some time for me," Maggie said as she came up behind him.

"I've always got time for you, Maggie. Where would you like to talk?" Daniel questioned with a smile. He seemed much happier these days, and Maggie was more than a little aware of his interest in Lillie.

"Well, talking is only part of what I have in mind," Maggie began, rather embarrassed by the situation. She followed him to the corral and opened the gate for him. "I need to see you as a patient."

"Is something wrong?" Daniel questioned, and the concern in his voice touched Maggie. He took the rope from the bay's neck and gave him a light smack on the rump. The horse moved quickly across the corral and Maggie waited while Daniel secured the gate. He tossed the rope over the fence post and questioned Maggie again. "Are you sick?"

"No, not really. At least I don't think so." Maggie smiled and then leaned forward to whisper, "I think I'm expecting." Her face lit up at the thought of the child she hoped was growing inside.

A grin played at the corners of Daniel's lips. "Does Garrett know?"

"No. I didn't want to get his hopes up until I was sure. You know how much he wants children," Maggie said softly.

Daniel put his arm around Maggie as they walked toward the house.

"I don't know what you two are up to, but I see red when another man has his arm around my gal," Garrett called good-naturedly from where he stood talking to a ranch hand.

"Too bad!" Daniel called over his shoulder. "You can wait your turn. Right now, the lady prefers my company."

Maggie knew that Garrett would wonder about her silence, so she turned to ease his mind. "Daniel is going to show me what type of bandages he needs for the hospital. Lillie and I are going to roll him a whole wagon full."

"I guess I can't stand in the way of medicine." Garrett laughed and waved them off.

After a brief examination, Daniel gave Maggie the news that she'd hoped for. "You are definitely pregnant," he said with a smile. "I'd say you can expect this young 'un around the third week of January."

"Oh, Daniel," Maggie said, excitement coloring her voice. "I'm so happy, and I know Garrett will be, too. My only worry is Lillie."

"Lillie?" Daniel questioned. "Has she been feeling ill?"

"No, but you know how hard it is for her to think about her baby. I wonder what learning about this baby will do to her. I'd hate to be the cause for Lillie's pain, but I'm so happy I'd feel untrue to Garrett and myself if I handled it any other way," Maggie said thoughtfully.

"Of course you would, and Lillie wouldn't expect it any other way," Daniel said solemnly. "She may have difficulty with the announcement, but there's another four-and-a-half months to get adjusted to the idea."

"I suppose you're right. I guess I'd better just put it in God's hands and trust Him to take care of Lillie. He's given me a wonderful gift, and I'm not going to pretend that I'm not happy when I'm thrilled," Maggie said as she got to her feet. "Now if you'll excuse me, I have some news to tell my husband."

"I can well imagine what his reaction will be," Daniel said with a grin. "There'll be no way for him to get that black Stetson on that head of his, once it commences swelling with pride."

Maggie laughed and surprised Daniel with a hug. "I'm so glad we have you here, Daniel. I used to worry about what it would be like if I did have a baby out here without medical facilities, but with you here at the ranch, or at least as close as Bandelero, I know I'll be just fine. I'm so blessed that God brought you to us."

Daniel frowned over Maggie's shoulder. It wasn't her reference to God as much as his self-doubt that bothered him. Maggie was certain he'd be her deliverance in birthing the baby, but Daniel wasn't that convinced. He reminded himself silently that at the last two deliveries he'd attended, both mothers and babies had lost their lives.

Maggie turned to leave, not realizing Daniel's dilemma, but turned back briefly to question him again. "What kind of bandages will you be wanting Lillie and me to roll for you? I don't want to lie to Garrett."

Daniel's mind was still focused on his concerns for the blue-eyed woman that so innocently stood before him, willing to place her trust and life in his hands. She didn't look old enough to be married, Daniel mused, but then, neither had Katie.

Daniel took down a rolled bandage and handed it to Maggie. "About four inches wide, and the length can vary." His words were rather stiff, and Maggie mistook his tone for professionalism.

"Sounds simple enough," she replied. Then she added, "Are you coming along to hear Garrett's reaction?"

"No, you go on. I didn't get enough of a ride earlier, and I think I'm going to go back out. Would you mind telling Garrett, in case he wonders?" Daniel requested.

"Not at all, Daniel," Maggie said and left Daniel with a smile.

"So, are you done rolling bandages?" Garrett teased as he met Maggie coming down the hallway.

"Yes, as a matter of fact, I am," Maggie said with smile.

Garrett wrapped his arms around Maggie's waist and grimaced. "I think you took the weight off Lillie and put it on yourself. You know if you get too fat, I'll have to send you away," Garrett joked, and Maggie lifted questioning eyes to her husband's face.

"You wouldn't love me if I were fat?"

Garrett's face looked puzzled for a moment before he said, "Mrs. Lucas, I would love you if you were twice this size."

"Well, that's good," Maggie said with a teasing smile forming on her lips, "because I intend to get twice this size."

Garrett laughed out loud, still not understanding her meaning. "I don't think so, Mrs. Lucas. I'll lock you in your room first, and then we'll see how fat you get without a cupboard to raid ten times a day."

Maggie sighed, but the teasing was still in her voice. "As

long as you let Daniel come see me, say in about four-and-
a-half months," she whispered.

"Why, so you can roll more bandages?" Maggie's
teasing suddenly seemed to make sense to Garrett. "Wait
a minute," he said and set Maggie at arm's length. He
closely scrutinized her figure and her flushed face. "Are
you telling me that you're, that we—"

"That's right," Maggie laughed. "We're having a baby."

"I can't believe it," Garrett said laughing as he whirled
Maggie in a circle.

"Well believe it. Daniel says it's true. You were right.
We were up to more than just bandages," Maggie teased.
"Now put me down before you make me dizzy."

Garrett gently placed Maggie back on the ground and
kissed her soundly on the lips. "You've certainly made my
day, Magdelena," he whispered using her full name.

"What's going on?" Lillie asked as she came out of her
bedroom dressed in riding clothes.

Garrett squeezed Maggie's shoulders. "Hasn't Maggie
told you? I figured I was the last one to know."

"Told me what?" Lillie asked innocently, and Maggie
jabbed Garrett in the side. She'd hoped to tell Lillie when
they were alone.

"Maggie's having a baby," Garrett announced, still not
realizing that Maggie's discomfort was founded in fear of
Lillie's reaction.

"That's wonderful, Maggie," Lillie managed to say, but
the words were mechanical and Maggie knew her friend
was in serious pain.

"I wanted to tell you later when we could talk alone,"
Maggie said as she stepped forward to take Lillie's hand.

Lillie surprised them all by backing away. "I'm going

for a ride. I'd like to be alone. I'm sure you understand."
With that Lillie ran down the hallway.

"What was that all about?" Garrett asked his worried wife.

"I knew she wouldn't be able to handle it," Maggie said and started to cry. Garrett finally understood and took Maggie in his arms.

"Shhh," he whispered against Maggie's copper hair. "God will care for Lillie. Come on, we'll pray for her together."

Lillie barked out the commands for a horse and flew into the saddle before the cinch was tightened. She went blazing across the yard and headed toward the mountains. The memories of Jason and the baby barely surfaced through the anger and sorrow that filled her heart.

She's having a baby, she's having a baby! The words echoed in Lillie's ears. Her hat flew off her head and went in the opposite direction of her galloping steed. Lillie urged the horse faster and faster until the scenery was a blur.

In the back of her mind, Lillie became conscious of a voice. Someone calling her name. She turned slightly in the saddle to find a mounted Daniel, riding in a fury to catch up with her.

Lillie kicked the horse's flanks unmercifully and nearly lost control of the reins as the gelding picked up speed. There was no way on earth that she was going to deal with Dr. Monroe and any of his wisdom.

Ignoring Daniel as he cut across the field to head her off, Lillie glanced up in time to see a barbed wire fence directly in front of her. Lillie had been riding since she was very young and jumping fences was certainly nothing new to her. She leaned down on the neck of her horse and raised up slightly to hug her body against the gelding. This should have been enough to signal the horse that she was prepared for the jump, but it didn't work. Instead, the poor gelding, having never been required to jump fences, came to a complete stop at the edge of the barbed wire.

Lillie fought to keep her hold, but it was no use. Momentum threw her over the horse's head and into the razor-edged barbed wire.

Lillie's scream split the silence. Daniel was nearly a minute behind her, and when he managed to get to the fence, Lillie was thrashing wildly in the tangled broken fence.

"Lillie, stop moving," Daniel ordered as he came to her. "Did you hear me?"

"Get it off me. It's cutting me," Lillie said as she pushed at the wire with her bloodied hands. Her skirts were hopelessly intertwined with the wire, and Daniel knew the more Lillie thrashed, the worse things would be.

"Lillie, if you don't stop it, you're going to hurt yourself even more." Daniel reached out and took Lillie's hands in his own. She was crying, and her tears broke Daniel's heart in two.

"It hurts," Lillie sobbed, but she tried not to fight the wire.

"I know," he said softly. "Now, I want you to remain perfectly still while I see if I can't get you lose. Do you understand?

"Yes," Lillie whimpered.

Daniel tried to untangle the wire gently, but some of it was embedded in the cloth of Lillie's riding skirt. "I'm going to have to cut some of your skirt," Daniel said as he reached for his pocket knife.

As Daniel cut away the bloodied cloth of her skirt, Lillie could see that she was far from out of danger. The calves of her legs had been protected by her riding boots, but her knees and lower thighs had no such protection.

"Lillie, you're losing quite a bit of blood." Daniel's face was grave as he continued to work at freeing her. "I've got to get the bleeding to stop." Lillie nodded as she passed into unconsciousness.

When she woke up, Lillie was surprised to find herself back at the ranch house in Daniel's examining room.

"I see you're back among the living," Daniel said as he brought a tray of instruments and supplies.

"What are you going to do?" Lillie questioned fearfully.

"I'm going to clean the wounds on your legs, and then I'm going to stitch the ones that need it," he said never taking his eyes from the concoction that he was mixing.

"Stitch them? You mean with a needle?" Lillie questioned, swallowing hard. She wished she'd stayed unconscious.

"I don't know of another way," Daniel replied sternly. He was completely in charge, and his years of professional training were making themselves evident in his exacting actions.

"I don't think so," Lillie said as she tried to scoot up the table. She was mortified to find that her legs were exposed, while a sheet covered her lap.

"I don't remember giving you a choice," Daniel said as he looked up to see the fear in Lillie's eyes. "Relax, Lillie. I'm not going to hurt you. I have medication that will numb the pain. If I don't stitch the wounds, they'll start bleeding again."

"I don't want this," Lillie said as she pulled away.

Lillie cried out in pain as she struggled to move. Her legs felt like they were on fire, and for the first time she noticed the ugly red gashes that scarred her thighs and knees.

"Lillie, don't move," Daniel said as placed his hand on her calf. The action stilled Lillie immediately, but not for the reasons intended. Daniel's touch caused her mind to flood with confusing emotions.

Daniel stood fixed with his hand on his leg, and Lillie began to tremble as she looked into his eyes. He recognized the change in Lillie and remained silent. He reached up and touched her cheek as lightly as a feather. When she didn't grimace or pull back, Daniel allowed his hand to travel the length of her jaw.

Lillie couldn't explain the feelings inside her. She wanted to fight Daniel, to tell him not to touch her, but her mouth wouldn't make the words. Her eyes remained fixed to his, and when he lowered his mouth to hers, Lillie didn't fight. Instead, she found herself clinging to Daniel's neck as if he were offering her a lifeline.

The kiss lasted only a moment, but when Daniel pulled away, Lillie saw none of the teasing or sarcasm that she knew him well capable of. She was inundated with varying emotions. She felt guilty for having allowed Daniel to kiss her, but she also had enjoyed it. How could she do that to Jason? He'd been the love of her life, and she had sworn to love no other. The words of her marriage vows came back to haunt her: Till death do us part.

Lillie realized she wasn't bound to Jason by anything earthly, but in her heart she'd thought it impossible to ever love again. Her eyes narrowed silently and Daniel glanced at her to find a very determined look on her face.

"If you're thinking of running away, it won't do you any good," he said to break the tension. His mind cried out at the betrayal of his long dead, Katie. But was it betrayal? he wondered.

"I don't want any more pain," Lillie said, with two-fold meaning.

"I know," Daniel said softly. "That's why I mixed this up. It'll take away the pain in your legs. I promise that if you're still in pain after drinking this, I won't touch your legs."

Lillie looked suspiciously at Daniel and then at the glass he held. "I don't know," she began, but Daniel was already lifting the glass to her lips.

"Just drink it, Lillie. Then while we wait you can tell me why you were riding that horse like a crazed fool."

Thou fool, this night thy soul shall be required of thee. The words of Luke came back to haunt Lillie's thoughts. Fear filled her eyes as she felt warmth spread through her body. She gripped Daniel's arm.

"Am I going to die?" The words were out of her mouth before Lillie realized what she'd said.

Daniel sensed the anguish and fear. He reached out and pulled Lillie into his arms and cradled her gently. "Of course not, Lillie."

"I was a fool, Daniel. I couldn't bear the news that

Maggie was with child. I was so selfish in my own pain, but I had to get away from here. I couldn't stand it." Lillie thought her words sounded slurred.

"I know. I know," Daniel reassured. "I have my own reasons for fearing Maggie's condition," he said honestly.

Lillie's eyes opened wide, in childlike amazement. "You do?" The question was barely whispered.

"I lost my wife in childbirth, the baby, too. I was their only medical help, and although I'd had the finest university training, I couldn't save them." Daniel's pain was clear.

"You know then," Lillie murmured. "You know about the nightmares and the pain."

Daniel ached at the longing and need voiced in Lillie's words. "Yes," he said as he stroked her hair.

"Daniel, I must be dying. I can't stay awake," Lillie said sadly, but the fear was no longer in her voice. Before he could reply, Lillie spoke again. "Daniel, do you think God hates me?"

"No," Daniel said painfully. How clever of God to deal with him through Lillie; deal with him in a way that he couldn't escape.

"I think He does, Daniel," Lillie said as her eyelids fought the heaviness. "I blamed Him for everything, and I know He hates me. That's why I'm dying."

"Hush, Lillie you are not dying. I just gave you a sleeping powder."

"You hate me, too, don't you?" Lillie struggled to ask the question before finally slipping into unconsciousness.

"Nothing could be further from the truth, Lillie. Nothing."

ten

"But I don't want to stay in bed anymore," Lillie announced to Daniel.

"If I let you get up, you'll just run around and tear open those stitches. Be patient, and I'll take the stitches out in another few days."

"If the stitches are coming out in a few days anyway, why can't I get up?" Lillie demanded.

"Because I'm the doctor and I said no." With that Daniel left the room, passing Garrett in the doorway as he left.

"She's not to get out of that bed, and if she tells you otherwise, she's lying," Daniel told Garrett.

Garrett laughed. "Is she being that bad?"

"Worse. I wouldn't go in there unless you're prepared for a battle. Boredom has made her mean."

Garrett glanced past Daniel, where Lillie sat with an indignant look on her face. "I see what you mean. I'll be careful." Daniel shrugged his shoulders and walked down the hall.

"How are you feeling, Lillie?" Garrett questioned as he took a seat in the chair beside Lillie's bed.

"I'm tired of being in this bed," Lillie answered. "Daniel still won't let me get up. It isn't fair."

"Life's not fair, Lillie. Nobody promised that it would be. Jesus said we'd have trials and tribulation," Garrett said trying hard to find a way to talk to Lillie about God. Maggie's concerns for her best friend had quickly become

Garrett's concerns as well.

"Then why try?" Lillie asked.

"What's the alternative? We can give up and spend our time in misery and discomfort, but that's not what God has in mind."

"How do you know? Maybe God doesn't like us or maybe He's mad because we've done something we shouldn't. Churches are always telling us what sinners we are," Lillie said, realizing that she cared more about the conversation than she'd originally thought she would.

"We are sinners," Garrett began. "That much is true. But God gave us a way to be forgiven. Jesus came to this earth and died for those sins."

"Surely He died for his friends and family, or for the people of his time. I can't believe He died for those who hadn't been born."

"But that's what's so special about it, Lillie. He did die for you. A long time ago, Jesus looked down through history and saw you and me, Maggie, Daniel, and everyone else, and He knew that we couldn't make it alone."

"But I feel alone," Lillie admitted sadly.

"I know you do, Lillie. That's because you don't have Jesus. None of us ever belongs until we repent of our sins and belong to Him. None of us heals until we let Him take control of our wounds."

"How can you be sure that God cares? How can you know whether He's listening to you or not?" Lillie questioned.

Garrett smiled knowingly. What Christian hadn't asked these same questions? Of course there were those fortunate few who found faith and trust in God an easy thing.

"It's a matter of faith, Lillie. When you finally come to

terms with the truth about Jesus Christ, nothing else matters. The pain, the fears, the denial—none of it matters anymore. It all falls away like the Scripture says. The old is passed away, and we become new creatures in Christ."

"Do you believe that, Garrett?"

"I sure do, Lillie. I believe it enough to stake my life on it," Garrett answered with firm assurance.

"I must say you've given me a great deal to consider," Lillie said thoughtfully. "If you don't mind, I'd like to take a nap now."

"Sure, Lillie." Garrett got up to leave, and then turned to add, "Lillie, just remember there's nothing so bad that God can't forgive it and forget it."

"How can anyone forget something like the wrongs in our life?" Lillie still couldn't bring herself to use the word *sin*.

"That's the joy of the God we serve, Lillie. The Bible says that He takes our sins and casts them into the sea of forgetfulness and remembers them no more. Now you try to get some rest, and I'll send Maggie to check up on you in an hour or two."

While Garrett had worked to show Lillie the plan of salvation, Maggie had sought out Daniel in order to ease his mind about her condition.

"Is something wrong? Are you feeling all right?" Daniel questioned as he joined Maggie in the courtyard.

"I'm fine, Daniel. I wanted to talk to you."

Daniel's worry still furrowed his brow. "I don't mean to cause you any distress, but in all honesty I'm not sure that I'm up to this challenge," he said as he settled into a cushioned, wrought iron chair. "I was thinking of leaving when Lillie had her accident."

"Daniel, no!" Maggie exclaimed. "You can't leave."

"I don't intend to, Maggie. I considered it long and hard, though."

"And?"

"And I've never been the kind of man who could run from a challenge. I pray I can do justice to your faith in me."

"Daniel, you're a fine doctor. I have the utmost confidence in you," Maggie said sincerely. "I'm so thankful you're here."

Daniel studied Maggie's face for a moment. She was radiant in her expectancy. Daniel remembered another radiant face, so petite and lovely, but that had been a lifetime ago.

"And I'm grateful for your confidence, Maggie. I can see why Garrett loves you so. Thank you for believing in me," Daniel said with a smile. In his mind, however, was the fervent hope that he could come to be as certain of his abilities as Maggie was.

Nearly a month had passed since Lillie's accident. She traced the pattern of the barbed wire scars and frowned. Once her beauty had been unmarred and she'd been so very proud of it. Now it seemed rather unimportant. Lying in bed all those days had given Lillie time to consider her life.

Beauty was so fleeting. One minute her body had been youthful, unscarred, innocent in nearly every way, and then she'd almost lost her life in the carriage accident. Scars had formed from that day on, and they only seemed to grow deeper. Scars upon scars.

Lillie pulled on two layers of petticoats to ward off the

dampness of the October rain. She was grateful for the clothing that Maggie had lent her and eagerly went to the closet to find something warm.

After pulling on a dark blue, wool dress, Lillie began to brush out her hair. She stared for a moment at the image in the mirror. Her hair now fell to the middle of her back. Funny, she thought, after cutting her hair she'd actually liked the unconventional shortness of it. She brushed her hair over and over until it gleamed from the attention, then braided it down the back and tied it with a blue ribbon.

After this was accomplished, Lillie secured the buttons that lined her sleeves from the wrist to the elbow. She'd always hated tedious tasks like these, but now it seemed that with each button, Lillie grew keenly aware of the chore. How often in life had she avoided seemingly tedious tasks simply because somebody else was at hand to do them for her?

Lillie sat down to pull on her high topped boots. With each turn of the button hook, Lillie realized that she'd missed out on many things in life. So much of her life had been consumed with material items and the value of those things. She laughed out loud when she thought that just a year ago she'd have found it offensive to be solely dependent upon a hand-me-down wardrobe. How different her life had become! Lillie finished with her shoes and went to stoke the fire in the kitchen stove.

"You're up awfully early," Daniel said from the shadows of the kitchen. He sat nursing a cup of coffee in the darkness.

"I wanted to build the fire up for breakfast, but I see you've already taken care of that," Lillie said rather shyly. Ever since Daniel had treated her wounded legs, Lillie felt extremely uncomfortable whenever she was alone with him. Lillie knew, however, that it hadn't been the touch of his hands on her legs, as much as the shared kiss that made her ill at ease. Ignoring her troublesome feelings, Lillie pulled a white apron from the cupboard and tied it securely around her tiny waist.

Daniel smiled appreciatively knowing that Lillie wouldn't be able to make out the details of his face. She was a handsome woman, and Daniel knew it was senseless to ignore the fact that she had come to haunt his thoughts both day and night.

"Have you eaten yet?" Lillie asked as she turned up the lamp. Her eyes met Daniel's for a moment. Daniel's steely blue eyes narrowed slightly as if contemplating Lillie's pale blue ones.

Lillie resisted the urge to reach out and touch the sandy hair that still looked slightly rumpled from sleep. Daniel wore a white, cotton shirt open at the neck, and Lillie could see that he'd rolled the sleeves up as if to prepare for some job. Lillie wanted to say something to break the spell, but instead, she turned away from Daniel's intense stare and went to the larder in search of bacon.

When Garrett and Maggie joined them, Lillie had already prepared bacon, fried potatoes, scrambled eggs, and biscuits.

"It sure smells good in here," Garrett drawled as he helped Maggie to a seat. Her well-rounded figure spoke of how close she was to giving birth.

"I'll say," Maggie added with enthusiasm. "I could eat a horse."

Daniel and Garrett laughed at this as Lillie placed a platter of food in front of Maggie. "There's no need to resort to horseflesh," Lillie said with a grin. "I don't think the baby would care for that near as well as he would for this."

"You never know," Maggie teased. "After all this is a Lucas baby."

"Just what is that suppose to mean?" Garrett questioned with a twinkle in his eye.

"Well, I—" Maggie's words fell silent at the shouting voices that came from the yard outside.

"What in world is going on?" Lillie said as she moved toward the kitchen.

"Stay here," Garrett instructed and motioned for Daniel to join him. "We'll check it out."

"Garrett, be careful," Maggie said with great concern for her husband.

Lillie put her arm around Maggie and gave her a reassuring hug. "We'll wait right here."

Garrett and Daniel soon returned, and the expression on their faces left the women without doubt that something serious was wrong.

"It's the Indian village. The Pueblos have a measle epidemic on their hands," Garrett said as he sat down beside his wife. "Daniel, you might as well eat breakfast first. You won't be able to do much good on an empty stomach."

"I suppose you're right," Daniel said as he sat down and picked up a biscuit.

"Let's join hands and pray," Garrett suggested and took hold of his wife's hand. "Father, we come to You to ask Your blessings and mercies," Garrett prayed. "I want to ask a particular blessing of wisdom upon Daniel as he prepares to work with Your children, the Pueblo. In James

1:5 you tell us 'If any of you lack wisdom, let him ask of God, that giveth to all men liberally.' Father, we need that wisdom now to deal with this measle epidemic and to keep it from spreading any farther. Amen."

"Amen," Maggie whispered.

For a moment an uncomfortable silence fell upon the four. Lillie refused to look up from her plate, and Daniel seemed preoccupied with the task at hand.

"You'll need some help," Garrett said as he dug into the plateful of food.

"I hadn't thought of that, but you're right. I suppose you're too busy to go, and Maggie certainly can't go," Daniel stated.

"Why don't you ask Jenny," Maggie suggested. "David and Jenny know most of the people. I'm sure she'd be more than happy to help you."

"No," Daniel said firmly and dismissed any possibility of argument.

Maggie heard the bitterness and anger in Daniel's voice and decided to drop the matter.

"Why can't I go and help?" Lillie suddenly questioned. "I've had the measles, and I'm healthy and strong."

"I don't think so Lillie," Daniel said, thinking of her life of ease and comfort. "I don't think you could keep up with the work."

"I have a great deal of determination, Dr. Monroe," Lillie said rather slighted. "I can do most anything I set my mind to. Tell me what to do, and you'll see that I'm made out of stronger stuff than you give me credit for."

"I think Lillie's right," Maggie affirmed. "She could be a great asset to you."

Daniel glanced curiously from Maggie to Lillie, and

finally to Garrett. At Garrett's nod, Daniel shrugged his shoulders.

"All right, Lillie can go along," Daniel answered the questioning looks of his three friends. "But I'm warning you, Lillie, it won't be easy and it won't be pretty. There will be a great deal of death and pain. Are you sure you're up to this?"

Ordinarily Lillie would have raged at anyone questioning her abilities, but she knew that Daniel understood what she'd been through. "I need to do this, Daniel." Her voice was soft, almost inaudible. How could she explain to the trio before her that she needed to do something unselfish and necessary. All her life, Lillie had been a lovely ornament, a lovely, useless ornament.

One look at her face, and Daniel nodded. "I understand, Lillie. Can you be ready to leave in ten minutes?"

"Of course," Lillie said as she got up from the table. "I'll go pack."

eleven

Lillie had never worked so hard in all her life. She was scarcely done with one patient when Daniel whisked her away to help with someone else.

Yellow Butterfly, a young Pueblo girl who'd once lived with David and Jenny Monroe, showed Lillie how to draw water from the river and carry it in the handmade pottery on top of her head. Lillie had to laugh amidst the gravity of the situation at her initial failed attempts.

As she made yet another trip back from the icy river, Lillie felt she would never see an end to the suffering and dying. She knelt beside an elderly Indian woman and began to bathe her feverish body with water. The woman's body was dotted from head to toe with telltale red spots.

The woman moaned and tried to speak, but Lillie hushed her with what little Tiwa dialect she'd learned from the Tanoan language that the Pueblo spoke.

Lillie spoke the words of reassurance over and over, but they paled in comparison to the effect her touch had on the old woman. Lillie gently stroked the graying hair of the woman as a mother would her child. The woman became quiet under Lillie's hand.

"Lillie!" It was Daniel calling her name from outside the adobe pueblo.

"I'm in here, Daniel," Lillie called as she left the old woman's side, the pot of water securely in hand.

"Are you holding up all right?" Daniel questioned,

exhaustion in his voice.

"I'm fine, but I think you'd better go back to the pueblo and get some sleep. If I need you, I'll wake you up," Lillie offered.

Daniel shook his head. "It isn't even noon yet."

"That hardly matters when you've been up all night," Lillie said sympathetically. "I promise I'll come get you if I need you."

Daniel pushed his hair back from his eyes, and for once the action didn't remind Lillie of her dead husband. "All right. I'll take a short nap, but you wake me by two o'clock."

"I think I can manage that," Lillie said with a slight smile. The truth was she could manage it, but she seriously doubted that she'd disturb Daniel once he got to sleep.

The afternoon sun had only warmed things marginally. Lillie had been so busy with her work that she hadn't noticed the hour, and with the first evening stars appearing in the sky, it was colder than ever.

With most of the sick resting peacefully, Lillie went to work alongside several Pueblo women who were washing out clothing and bedding. She stood over a caldron of boiling water, relishing the heat from the fire beneath it.

"Doctor Woman, come now," a young Indian girl said as she tugged at Lillie's skirt.

"What's wrong?" Lillie asked.

"Brother's sick. Bring medicine for baby. Come. Come now." The girl's urgency pushed Lillie into action.

Lillie followed the girl, whose long black hair flew out from behind her as the Indian blanket she used for a coat fell away. Lillie had taken to using a blanket of her own for warmth, but she'd forgotten to grab it. She regretted her forgetfulness and was grateful to see the young girl race inside one of the nearby adobe buildings.

The interior was dimly lit as Lillie stepped inside. The pueblos were always poorly lit, but those that housed the sick remained dark for the sake of eyes made sensitive to light by the measles. As Lillie's eyes adjusted, she could see a young mother holding her baby in his cradle board.

"You make my baby well, Doctor Woman?" The woman asked the question with hopeful eyes, as well as with her words.

"May I hold the baby?" Lillie questioned and motioned to the woman her meaning. "I'll need to take him out."

"Yes, yes. Hold baby," the woman mimicked the words. "Hold baby. Make well." The mother began to undo the fastenings that held her small son in his cradle board.

Lillie took the infant in her arms. The child's body was limp and burning up with fever.

"I must take him to the doctor," Lillie said as she took a blanket that hung on a nearby chair.

"Cries at Dawn go with you. You tell doctor, make baby well," the mother said and motioned her young daughter to follow Lillie.

Lillie cradled the baby to her chest and raced through the village. She and Daniel shared a three-room pueblo with the t'aikabede, the Pueblo tribal leader, at the opposite end of the village.

Cries at Dawn was at Lillie's heels as she entered the pueblo and called for Daniel. She hurried to the room where Daniel was jumping, fully clothed from the make-shift bed where he'd slept.

"Bring him here," Daniel instructed.

Lillie came forward and handed the infant to Daniel,

while Cries at Dawn looked on from the doorway. Daniel examined the infant briefly and shook his head. "I'm afraid he's gone."

The color drained from Lillie's face. She reached one hand out to the adobe wall to steady herself, while the other hand went to her mouth.

Daniel looked up to see Lillie's reaction. "Lillie, are you all right?" He wrapped the baby and handed him to Cries at Dawn. Daniel spoke in Tiwa to the girl. She cried softly as she held her brother close. He felt a certain responsibility to go with the child, but he knew that Lillie needed him more.

Daniel returned to the room where Lillie still stood against the wall. Grief had muted her, and the passing of the child in her arms was too much to comprehend.

Daniel pulled blankets from his bed and put one around Lillie's shoulders and the other around his own. Lillie offered no resistance as he led her from the house and down a worn pathway through the village.

Lillie felt numb from the death of the baby. She scarcely felt the cold night air as the blanket slipped from her shoulders. Daniel paused long enough to pull the blanket back around Lillie before moving from the path and into the canopy veil of pine and juniper trees.

Emerging from the trees, Lillie caught the sound of a waterfall. It awakened her mind from it's sorrowful hauntings and brought her back to the present.

"Where are we?" Lillie questioned softly, afraid to break the melodic ripplings that engulfed everything around her.

"This is Sacred Lake. The Pueblo hold this place in the highest esteem. They believe their strength and wisdom comes from here." Daniel moved along a rocky pathway that led them ever upward toward the sound of the water.

"But I don't see any lake," Lillie said as she strained in all directions to catch a glimpse of the water.

"You will," Daniel said as he reached back and took Lillie's hand. "Come on."

Lillie caught her breath in wonder when they reached the trail's end. The waterfall plummeted in splendor before them, and the moonlight glimmered as a thousand twinkling lights wherever it touched the icy crystals of frozen water.

"I thought you'd like it," Daniel said with a smile.

"I've never known anything more beautiful," Lillie said in complete honesty.

The water made a lyrical roar as it fell some seventy feet into Sacred Lake. Against the moon, the falls looked like a glimmering black ribbon as it twisted and cascaded toward the bottom. Sacred Lake stood out amidst the pillars of pine and reminded Lillie of black onyx.

"I had to share this with you. The t'aikabede told me of this place. He said that he came here often to offer up prayers to the Cloud People and the Corn Mother for a bountiful harvest. He said that this place had special healing powers and his people come here to bring corn-meal offerings for the blessings they seek."

"You've certainly learned a great deal about this place," Lillie said absentmindedly.

"I think this entire experience has taught me things about myself. Things that I'd let myself forget or ignore," Daniel remarked.

Lillie suddenly realized that Daniel was still holding her hand. His hand felt warm and strong against hers, and she felt guilty for never wanting Daniel to let go.

"Tell me about your wife," Lillie said without understanding why.

Daniel smiled and the faraway look in his eyes left Lillie little doubt of the deep love he felt for his long-departed wife.

"Katie was a lot like you," Daniel began. "She was delicate and petite, yet she had strength in her that I don't think she knew about. She was kind, loving, and gentle with nearly every living soul. However," Daniel paused and a grin spread across his face, "she had a temper and a stubborn streak that could match yours any day."

Lillie laughed out loud at this. "So you think I'm temperamental and stubborn. Is that it?"

"I don't just think it; I know it. Stubbornness has caused both of us a great deal of grief. Don't you agree?"

"I've always been used to having my own way," Lillie said thoughtfully. "However, my determination has often seen me through difficult times. Times that I might not otherwise have found my way through."

"Like when you lost your husband?" Daniel dared the question.

"Yes," she whispered. "I felt that Jason's death was my fault. I couldn't abide the fact that he'd given his life to God, when he'd promised to share it with me. I didn't understand that a person could do both. I didn't see in time, to really set Jason's mind at ease."

"When Katie died, I blamed God, as well as myself. She put such trust in my abilities, and when she knew I couldn't save her, she died with words of love for me. The last thing she said was that she loved me," Daniel uttered the words as a bittersweet eulogy.

Lillie said nothing for several moments. When she did speak, tears dampened her eyes. "I've never understood why God would allow things to happen as He did. It was easy to blame God for the pain because all my life I'd heard how much I'd wronged Him and how far from the mark of perfection I was in His eyes." Lillie paused for a moment remembering the words Garrett had shared with her when she'd been recuperating from her fall. "I'm beginning to see that maybe Garrett was right. Life happens. It isn't always what we hope it will be, and it isn't always what we need it to be. But God is always in it. Somehow I need to trust more and question less."

"That's very wise, Lillie. My brother David would say that you've come to an understanding of faith." Daniel's words echoed in his own mind. David had tried so patiently and lovingly to bring Daniel back to God, and now a woman who barely had hope enough to consider God's promises was guiding him back to an understanding of where he'd gone wrong. "Faith is the hard part. You want to believe, you pray to believe, and then when things fall down around you—sometimes you can't believe. That's where faith takes over and let's you believe even when the rest of the world says you're crazy."

"Do you think faith will get you through the bad times?" Lillie asked innocently.

Daniel gazed deeply into Lillie's huge, blue saucer eyes. He reached his hand up to touch her windblown cheek. "Yes, Lillie. I do believe that. I didn't realize until now that I still did. But faith is absolutely all I've had with me these years. Faith that the pain would go away, faith that my confidence would return, and even faith that God would send me another companion."

Lillie thought of Jason, but the memory had dimmed with time. Was it wrong to imagine that perhaps Daniel's faith had brought him to her? Was it wrong to hope that God had planned their meeting all along?

"David tried to help me after Katie passed away," Daniel added. "But I blamed him because he'd led me to salvation and to trust in God. I blamed David for Katie's death because he prayed for her and told me that God could make things right. When Katie died, David told me that God must have other plans for my life and that Katie had only been a short, special part of those plans. I hated him for saying that, Lillie. I hated my own brother for the comfort he tried to give me. I felt that his God had taken my Katie and my unborn child; therefore I hated both God and David."

"I know," Lillie breathed. "I felt the same about Jason and his God. I couldn't bear being replaced in Jason's life by a faceless image that I knew nothing about."

Daniel nodded his head in understanding. His hand continued to stroke Lillie's cheek as he contemplated her words.

Lillie found her free hand voluntarily going up to her face to hold Daniel's hand against her cheek. How she longed to be held. "Please," she whispered in the stillness that surrounded them, "please hold me."

Daniel didn't need to be asked more than once. His arms pulled Lillie against him and held her tightly. It wasn't Katie that he thought of, and for the first time since his wife's death, it wasn't Katie that he wanted to hold. It was Lillie.

Lillie clung to Daniel as though she were taking her very life's blood from the embrace. She felt a strengthening and a peace of mind that she'd not known herself capable of.

An owl hooted from the tall pines overhead, breaking the spell of silence that shrouded them. Lillie pulled away slightly, just enough to see Daniel's face. His expression was one of peace and something else that Lillie didn't understand.

"What is it?" she asked as she reached up to touch his hair.

"I just asked God to forgive me for being so stubborn," Daniel said and the joy in his voice was evident with each word. "Lillie, I'm free again. Free from the past and the pain. Free from blaming God and my brother. I know it sounds incredible, but faith is exactly what has been missing in my life. Until now I could never put a name to it."

"How do you know God will listen? How do you know that you're forgiven?" Lillie questioned.

Daniel took Lillie's face in his hands, and his blanket dropped unheeded to the ground. "I know because He promised He would in the Bible. I chose to ignore Him and trust circumstances and emotions rather than His promises. But one thing I know now is that God's peace is never conditional upon my surroundings or the events in my life. God's peace is always with me. Jesus promised it, and my faith in that will sustain me through any circumstance."

"How I wish I could be as certain as you are," Lillie replied as she contemplated Daniel's declaration.

"I'm going to pray that God will send you that peace, Lillie. I'm going to pray, too, that you will be able to free yourself from the past and look to a new future."

Daniel's words seemed to hint of something more. Could he mean a future with him? Before Lillie could ask

Daniel what he meant, he kissed her, silencing all her questions.

twelve

With Christmas only a week away, Lillie and Daniel packed the last remnants of their supplies and said good-bye to the t'aikabede. The Pueblos were well on their way to recovering from the measle epidemic, although the fresh mounds of dirt revealed the losses the tribe had sustained.

The entire village turned out to wave goodbye to Doctor and Doctor Woman, as Lillie had come to be called. She enjoyed helping the Pueblo people and was giving serious consideration to becoming a nurse.

A half-day's ride east took Daniel and Lillie to the home of Jenny and David Monroe. Before Lillie and Daniel had ridden into view, David and Jenny stood at the fence post, shocked and surprised.

"You must be Lillie," Jenny said as she took Lillie in hand. "I feel I know you. Maggie has shared so many wonderful things about you." Lillie was dumbfounded by the bubbling and vivacious Jenny Monroe.

As Daniel watched Lillie disappear he was greeted with a hearty bear hug from his younger brother.

"Dan," David said near to tears. "I thank God you've come home."

"Yes, indeed," Daniel said in agreement. "I've come home to God and to you. Can you forgive me for the past, little brother?"

"Don't you already know the answer to that?" David

questioned with a laugh. "I've prayed long and hard for this moment. Jenny, too. I'm sorry to say, she had more faith about it happening than I did."

"I didn't give you a reason to have much faith, but the issue of faith is what brought me to a spirit of willingness," Daniel said honestly as he put his arm around his brother.

They were two of kind, tall, lean, and tan. Yet there were subtle differences in the two men. Daniel had always been the prankster of the two, and it showed in the laugh lines that edged his eyes. David had always been more serious. It was this seriousness and need to understand the deep secrets of God that led David into the ministry. Yet for all their differences, they were brothers.

Jenny had swept Lillie into the house and had managed to put a cup of hot coffee in Lillie's hands before she knew what had happened.

"All I can say is that it's wonderful to have you both here," David announced as he and Daniel joined them at the table. He motioned for Daniel to sit between him and Lillie and smiled broadly as Daniel accepted the offered chair. Jenny put out a pot of coffee and a large platter of cookies.

"I'd like to offer a word of thanks," David said as he took hold of Jenny's hand, "that is if no one has any objections."

"Not as far as I'm concerned," Daniel replied as he took David's offered hand. Daniel extended his other hand to Lillie.

Lillie felt her heart quicken as she reached out for Daniel's hand. She hoped that her eyes didn't betray her emotions.

Daniel might not have noticed Lillie's face, but Jenny did. She took Lillie's free hand and gave it a heartfelt squeeze. When Lillie cast a glance at Jenny, the loving warmth in Jenny's eyes was apparent.

"Let's pray," David said softly, and all four bowed their heads. "Father, today we offer thanksgiving for answered prayer. You told us that the Good Shepherd leaves the ninety-nine to search for the one lost sheep. Today you have sought and found the lost and brought him safely back into the fold. For this Lord, we praise and honor You; giving You the glory forever and ever. Amen."

Lillie looked up to find that Jenny and David had tears in their eyes. Further inspection revealed that Daniel, too, had dampness on his cheeks. Lillie felt as if she were an outsider.

For the rest of the day, Lillie considered the encounter at the Monroe kitchen table. She was confused and empty, wanting to understand what the others knew yet fearing it at the same time. She was sitting alone in the bedroom that Jenny had given her when a knock sounded on the door.

"Lillie, it's me, Jenny. May I come in?"

"Of course, Jenny."

Jenny opened the door only a crack. "If this is a bad time I can come back later."

"No. Please stay," Lillie said as she got up and opened the door wide.

"Would you like to go for a walk? I know it's kind of cold outside, but I need to take care of some things in the barn," Jenny said with an openness that Lillie couldn't ignore.

"I'd love to," Lillie admitted. "I must admit that I was growing rather bored with myself. Too much time to think and all. Does that make any sense?"

"It makes perfect sense," Jenny said kindly. "Come on."

The crisp December wind stung Lillie's face and eyes.

She pulled her cape closer and wished that she'd thought to add one of the warmer Indian blankets.

"This is a much colder winter than most," Jenny said as she led Lillie away from the house. "I can't abide it when it turns so bitterly cold. Was it this cold in Kansas?"

"Colder. In Kansas the cold is so often accompanied by rain or very wet snow. You can never get warm or dry," Lillie said, and her mind flashed back to the cold dampness of her nightmare. Funny, she hadn't noticed when the dreams had stopped plaguing her.

The barn was adobe like the house. Inside, Lillie was amazed at how warm and comfortable it was. Jenny also kept a root cellar in the barn and stored many of her provisions. After filling her basket with jars of canned vegetables and meat, Jenny suggested that they take a different way back to the house.

"I know I'm getting rather personal, but I couldn't help noticing the way you reacted when Dan touched you. I was hoping that maybe God threw you two together for companionship. Is that too painful to discuss with me?" Jenny asked honestly.

Lillie stared at the ground as she answered. "I don't know that painful is the right word. I find myself confused more than anything."

"Why not talk with a friend then?" Jenny suggested.

"I guess I would like to talk to someone," Lillie admitted. "I don't want to burden Maggie, not with her baby coming so soon. I wouldn't want to do anything to jeopardize that child arriving safely into the world."

"Maggie told me about your husband and baby's deaths," Jenny said as she took hold of Lillie's arm. "You still pine for them, don't you?"

Lillie lifted her face to meet Jenny's companionate eyes. "Yes, more than you'll ever know."

"I understand quite well, Lillie. I lost three babies myself."

Lillie gasped unable to hide her shock. "Three? How did you make it?"

"It wasn't easy, even with my confidence and faith in God. I was hurt and angry. When I lost my first baby, I stepped back and said, 'It's the will of God. I can accept this.' The second time, I was more devastated than the first. I was so certain that nothing could go wrong because the worst had already happened. I was wrong. Things got worse. I wanted to rant and rave at God. I couldn't understand why He would let something like this happen. I wish I could say my faith got me through, but God's compassion took over and numbed my pain, giving me a chance to work through the grief."

"Then what happened?" Lillie questioned, wanting and needing to know how this young woman had sustained her soul through these crises.

"My last baby was due about this time two years ago. Things had gone fairly well, and I was starting to feel confident again. I went into labor, gladly suffering the pain in order to have the child I longed for. I gave birth to a son. He lived only a few hours. I don't know why he died. He looked healthy and strong, but I guess it wasn't meant to be. After that, there wasn't one shred of pride or arrogance left in me. I knew God was preparing my heart for something, but I couldn't figure out what I could possibly learn by losing my children."

Jenny's words echoed in Lillie's mind. Was God trying to prepare Lillie's heart for something as well?

"How could you still trust God after all that?" Lillie asked.

"How could I not? What other alternative did I have?" Jenny replied. "To turn away would mean disregarding all I knew to be true simply because I didn't get my own way. Committing to God means more than trusting Him for the good in life. It means trusting Him in the darkest valleys of life as well."

"I think I understand," Lillie answered. Garrett's words blended with Daniel's and Jenny's were helping her make more sense out of the things Jason had tried to share with her before he died.

"Just remember, Lillie. God doesn't leave you in the dark. He doesn't forsake you and allow you to wander blindly. If you seek Him, He'll lead you back to the light."

"It's so much to take in," Lillie said as she pulled her cloak tight. The wind buffeted both women until their cheeks were rosy and tender.

Jenny laughed heartily as they made their way back to the house. "That's true, Lillie. But it has been my experience to find God faithful at every turn. I don't have my own children with me, but look at the family I have by way of the Pueblos. There are eight children living with us at this time. Sometimes there are more, sometimes less, but always there is someone in need. God sent these children to me because He knew we needed each other. I think that's why you and Daniel found each other as well."

"I never thought of it that way. I saw Daniel as a nuisance at first. He ridiculed my overeating and made fun of my weight. Then he seemed to pop up wherever I went and that truly annoyed me," Lillie stated firmly, then added, "at first."

"Why do you suppose it annoyed you so much?"

Lillie laughed. "I've often asked myself the same question. I'm still not sure I know, but he doesn't bother me near as much as he used to."

Jenny smiled. "I've noticed."

Lillie looked shocked. "I didn't mean anything by it. I mean my husband hasn't even been gone a year. I don't have a right to have feelings for anyone else."

"And why not?" Jenny's tone sounded indignant. "Because society says so, or because your heart says so?"

"I suppose because of society. Saying that bothers me more than you'll ever know. I feel guilty because I seldom think of Jason at all." Lillie's words were full of sadness. "I try to remember things, but the memories are clouded and vague. Then I feel guilty for not being able to remember."

"Lillie you mustn't feel guilty. You aren't under any obligation to your husband. That ended at the grave. Forgetting helps to buffer the loss and allows you to heal. You won't ever forget him totally. Just like Daniel will always remember Katie."

"Do you think it's all right then?" Lillie dared to ask the question that had haunted her heart for weeks. "Do you think it's all right to care about Daniel?"

The two women stopped at the kitchen door, noticing through the window that Daniel and David sat talking at the kitchen table. "I think it's more than all right, Lillie. I think it's what God has intended all along. I think it's His way of healing you both."

Lillie thought about Jenny's words long after she'd dressed for bed that night. One thing seemed clear:

happiness had little to do with material things or a full social calendar.

Lillie had lived quite simply in the Indian village, and mission life could certainly not compare to that which she'd known back in Topeka. Yet, Lillie was certain she'd never felt more at peace. If only she could work through her feelings about God. She wanted to believe the things that everyone had told her. She knew that Daniel was much happier since he'd made his peace with God.

Snuggling deeper into the layers of blankets, Lillie thought of Jenny Monroe's contented look as she had shared with Lillie about her life at the mission. Jenny mothered the Indian children as if they were her own, and Lillie knew that children loved Jenny in return. If God had given Jenny peace of mind after losing three babies, surely He could give Lillie peace of mind after losing just one. Lillie comforted herself with the thought as she fell into a much needed sleep.

Jenny was already busy with the children when Lillie came down for breakfast. Jenny was combing hair and dressing little bodies, all the while laughing and singing with the children. "You go ahead and get some breakfast. We have our routine, and we'll be just fine," Jenny called out to Lillie.

Lillie suppressed a giggle at the sight of the wiggling toddlers who seemed to mess their hair up as soon as Jenny had combed it. She was still laughing to herself as she entered the kitchen to find Daniel eating breakfast.

"You certainly look happy," Daniel said as he got up to offer Lillie a seat.

"I actually feel happy," Lillie said as she took the offered chair.

Daniel silently appraised the trim, blond woman. It was useless to deny the feelings that he had for her. Just the scent of her perfume took his mind back to the first time he'd met her. She had been so angry and vulnerable.

Daniel took his seat at the table and wondered silently if Lillie could ever care for him as much as he cared for her.

"Whatever are you smiling about?" Lillie asked with a grin. The morning happiness at the mission was contagious.

Daniel stared at her with a quizzical look. Should he say something? He toyed with the idea for only a moment before deciding against saying anything that might scare Lillie off. Instead he shrugged his shoulders and passed Lillie a platter full of biscuits.

In the other room the musical laughter of children rang throughout the house. "They're certainly a lively bunch," Lillie commented as she helped herself to some bacon. "Jenny's a lucky woman."

"Why do you say that?" Daniel asked.

Lillie put her fork down and stared thoughtfully for a moment. "I guess because she has a mate and children and a home." Lillie's honesty surprised them both.

"Is that what you want out of life, Lillie?"

Lillie met Daniel's stare. She lost herself for a moment in his eyes. Could she tell him how she felt? Should she?

Lillie trembled from the intensity of the moment. Her heartbeat quickened as she confronted the truth. "I never used to think that it would be enough. I wanted the money, the parties, and all the beautiful things that went with that lifestyle." She barely whispered the words loud enough to be heard.

"And now?" Daniel questioned, the urgency in his voice

clear. He reached out and placed his hand on top of Lillie's. He could feel her tremble beneath his touch.

Lillie swallowed hard and looked down at the large, well-manicured hand that covered hers. The hand of a doctor, the hand of the most intriguing man she'd ever known. "It would be enough," Lillie answered and quickly removed her hand from beneath Daniel's.

Daniel started to say something, but Jenny came bursting into the room. "I hope you found enough to eat," Jenny said as she scrutinized the food on the table.

"We did, and it was wonderful," Lillie said as she concentrated on her plate to avoid Daniel's eyes.

"I'm glad you liked it. Daniel tells me that you two will have to be leaving this morning. Are you sure you can't stay longer?" Jenny asked as she cleared the empty dishes from the table.

Lillie hadn't realized that Daniel planned for them to leave so soon, but there was nothing to be gained by arguing. "I'd love to stay, but Maggie only has a month or so until the baby's due. I need to be there for her," Lillie replied as she finished her breakfast.

"Of course," Jenny said with a sad smile that Lillie understood full well. As happy as they both were for Maggie, there was the bittersweet reminder of the little ones they had lost. "I wish I could come and help, but as you know I have my hands full. Why, just trying to school the older children is a full-time job. But Maggie's in good hands. She has you and our good Dr. Dan. She'll be just fine."

Daniel remained silent. The reminder of Maggie's upcoming delivery was an unwelcome thought. He'd managed to make things right between himself and God, and David as well, but he still doubted his ability to care properly for Maggie and her unborn child.

"Did you hear me Daniel?" Jenny said as she gave his shoulder a light shake.

"I'm sorry," Daniel said as he looked into Jenny's warm eyes.

"I told you not to make a stranger of yourself again. Bandelero isn't all that far from here, and rumor has it that you're building an office and infirmary. So remember how to get here and bring Lillie back as soon as Maggie can spare her."

"I'll do that," Daniel promised. "But now, if Lillie is finished with her breakfast, we'll need to be getting back to the ranch."

Half an hour later, Lillie was bidding Jenny goodbye. "Don't forget what I told you, Lillie. God puts folks together for a reason."

"I'll remember," Lillie said with a smile and cast a glance toward Daniel who waited with the reins to her horse.

"I always know I'm in trouble when women share secrets and smiles," Daniel said as Lillie came toward him to accept his help into the saddle.

The cold leather creaked as Lillie settled into the seat. She gave Jenny a look of amusement and Jenny laughed as David came to stand beside her.

"If I didn't know better," David said from the ground, "I'd say you ladies were up to something."

Daniel stepped into the stirrup and threw his leg over, landing square in the seat of his saddle. "And just what makes you think that you know better, little brother? I'm convinced these ladies are up to something, but as of yet

I'm not convinced that it's to my detriment; so for the time being I'm going to wait them out."

thirteen

"Hurry, Lillie. Garrett and Daniel will be back with the tree any minute," Maggie called from the front sitting room. She put a hand to the small of her back and tried to rub away the soreness. She knew the action would achieve very little relief, but it had become such a habit that she continued to do it.

Lillie finally came down the hall carrying a small wooden crate. "Is this the right box?"

Maggie glanced up and smiled. "That's it. Don't you remember? These are the Christmas tree ornaments from my grandmother's house. You shipped them to me not long after she died."

Lillie placed the box on the lamp table and removed the lid. "Yes, I remember now," she said as she held up one of the delicate glass ornaments.

Maggie came and stood beside her friend. "I'm so glad you're here, Lillie. I've wanted to tell you so, but I didn't want to upset you. I want you to be comfortable and happy," Maggie said, placing her hand on Lillie's arm. "Are you all right? What with the baby coming and it being just last year. . . ." Maggie's voice fell silent.

Lillie put the ornament back in the box and turned to hug Maggie. "I'm fine. I don't know if it's God's grace like Jenny said, or just time and healing, but I've grown quite comfortable here. I just hope I haven't worn out my welcome. At least Daniel's been spending most of his time in Bandelero getting the hospital set up."

"Shame on you Lillie, for even thinking such a thing. This is your home for as long as you want it to be. I speak for myself as well as for Garrett. He told me just the other day that his mind was put at ease knowing that there'd be another woman in the house. Ever since Maria left for Santa Fe to care for her sick mother, Garrett's been a nervous wreck. He couldn't wait for you and Daniel to get back."

The sound of the wagon signaled the return of the men. Maggie moved toward the door, but Lillie put a hand on her shoulder. "Stay put. There is nothing you can do to help carry that tree in. I'll help them, and you just boss the rest of us around."

Maggie frowned. "I'm not an invalid," she called out to Lillie's retreating form. "I don't see any reason to sit here like some kind of ornament!" She might not be able to help with the tree, but there was certainly no reason that she couldn't make them a batch of cocoa.

Maggie made her way to the kitchen and began gathering the things she'd need. The milk was easy enough, as were the sugar and vanilla. It was the cocoa that eluded Maggie.

"Now where in the world did I put it?" Maggie muttered as she tore through the cupboards. After searching through all the lower shelves, Maggie had no alternative but to climb up on a chair to search the top shelf.

This ought to get me into a great deal of trouble if Garrett catches me, Maggie thought. Nonetheless, she hiked up her skirts and struggled to balance her weight enough to get up on the chair.

In the front room, Garrett and Daniel eased the freshly

cut pine tree into a metal bucket of sand and dirt. Lillie had helped guide the base of the trunk into the bucket and turned to ask Maggie's opinion of whether the tree was straight or not when she noticed that Maggie wasn't even in the room.

"Where's Maggie?" Lillie asked Garrett.

"I don't know. I just know that she's not manhandling this tree like she'd like to, so I'm hoping that she's staying out of trouble." The words were barely out of Garrett's mouth when a loud crash from the kitchen caused him to drop the tree and go in search of it's source.

Garrett first noticed the jar of peaches that had shattered in streaks of orange across the floor. Then he noticed his wife standing on the chair, looking surprised. "Magdelena Lucas! What in the world do you think you're doing?" Garrett questioned as he lifted Maggie into his arms and off the chair.

"I was going to make us some cocoa. I wanted to add something nice to our party. Now put me down, I have a mess to clean up," Maggie insisted, but Garrett held her all the more tightly.

"I'll clean it up myself, and you're going to sit down and behave yourself," Garrett said as he turned to take Maggie back to the sitting room. Lillie and Daniel stood in the doorway shaking their heads.

"Lillie, make Garrett put me down. Come help me," Maggie called out.

"No chance of that," Lillie replied as Garrett disappeared from the hallway. "I seem to recall asking you for help once upon a time when I was being held captive," Lillie's teasing voice made Daniel laugh.

"I don't think you minded the captivity as much as you

claimed," he said as Lillie went to retrieve the mop.

"Oh? You think you know everything don't you?" Lillie said trying to sound quite solemn.

"I think I know you pretty well," Daniel retorted.

She paused by the stove for a moment and the merriment of the moment got the best of her. She picked up the same cast iron skillet that she'd once chased after Daniel with. Turning to meet his amused stare, Lillie smiled.

"There seems to be some unsettled business between us, I recall."

Daniel stepped forward, undaunted by the skillet. "And what would that be?" he questioned as he closed the distance between them. Reaching out, Daniel easily pinned Lillie's arms to her side.

Lillie's upturned face feigned a pout. Her eyes were still laughing, however, and Daniel enjoyed the familiarity between them. Freeing one of Lillie's arms, Daniel reached down and took the skillet from her hand. Placing it on the stove, Daniel turned back to Lillie and pulled her into his arms.

They stood face to face for a moment, and Lillie trembled in anticipation that Daniel would kiss her. Ever so gently, his lips met hers, leaving Lillie breathless from the touch. Jason never entered her thoughts.

The pleasure of the moment was almost too much to deal with. Lillie thought her heart would burst from the over-whelming pounding. When Daniel dared the liberty of kissing her twice, Lillie pushed weakly at his chest.

"Stop, I can't breathe," she whispered.

"Maybe you need a doctor," he murmured.

"I can't clean up that mess if you don't let me go," Lillie insisted. Her cheeks grew flushed from the intensity of

Daniel's nearness.

"No, I don't suppose you can," he said, refusing to give up his hold.

"What is it exactly that you want?" Lillie questioned teasingly.

"That's simple," Daniel said as he lowered his lips. "I want you."

Lillie felt her mind race at Daniel's reply. He wanted her, but what did that mean? She needed to know, but Daniel didn't seem to be of a mind to continue their conversation. Finally Lillie gathered her strength and broke free of the embrace.

Her eyes betrayed her willingness, making it clear to Daniel that he could easily possess her. But something in her resolve to put distance between them caused Daniel to refrain from pulling her back against him.

"I'll help you clean up," Daniel offered.

"No, I think I'd like a few minutes alone to gather my wits," Lillie said as she reached down to retrieve the pieces of broken glass. "Why don't you go see to Maggie?"

"All right," Daniel said with a shrug of his shoulders. "But you'd best treat me well, or you won't be getting any Christmas present from me."

Lillie looked up in shock, but Daniel had already left the room. Christmas present? she thought. Why didn't I think to get him a Christmas present?

The thought of Daniel giving her a gift when she had nothing to offer in return grieved Lillie. After wiping away the last traces of peach juice, she joined the others to help with the Christmas tree, her mind still contemplating a gift for Daniel.

Maggie was sitting quite properly on the high-backed,

red velvet sofa, while Garrett and Daniel took instructions from her as to where she wanted things placed on the tree. Lillie laughed and called her friend Queen Victoria.

The mood remained lighthearted and jovial while Daniel, Garrett, and Lillie finished dressing the tree. When the last candle had been attached to the pine boughs, Garrett took on the task of lighting each one.

"It's beautiful," Maggie declared.

"What did you expect?" Garrett asked as he came to take the seat beside Maggie. "I happen to be an expert at decorating Christmas trees."

"Is there anything you aren't an expert at?" Maggie questioned sardonically.

Garrett considered the question for a moment and then said with a laugh, "I can't think of a thing at the moment."

"Then you and Daniel should make a fine pair," Lillie quipped. "He thinks he knows it all, too.

Daniel leaned back against the whitewashed adobe wall and crossed his arms against his chest. He'd long ago traded in his city-styled suits for a more casual look, and Lillie was quite taken with the lean, attractive Dr. Monroe.

"This is a much happier Christmas than last year," Maggie said as she handed Garrett the family Bible. "I wasn't sure I could ever enjoy Christmas quite as much as I used to, but you've all made this year special. I don't think it would have been near as much fun without you."

"We have a great deal to be thankful for," Garrett replied as he took the Bible. "Good friends, a new doctor for the territory, a baby on the way, and prosperity. We have much, indeed, to thank God for."

Lillie grew sober in the wake of Maggie and Garrett's reflection. A shadow from the past crossed her brow, and turning from the others, Lillie pretended to busy herself with putting away the crates that had housed the tree ornaments.

"Don't worry about those, Lillie. Garrett is going to read the Christmas story," Maggie said and beckoned Lillie with her hand. "Come sit over here by the fire."

Lillie did as Maggie bade, but she couldn't get the spirit of the season that the others had.

" And it came to pass in those days, that there went out a decree from Caesar Augustus, that all the world should be taxed.'" Garrett continued reading from the second chapter of Luke, but Lillie had difficulty focusing on the words. Why couldn't she have the same peace as the others?

" And she brought forth her firstborn son, and wrapped him in swaddling clothes, and laid him in a manager; because there was no room for them in the inn."

Lillie shifted uncomfortably. She glanced up to find Daniel watching her. His expression was compassionate, and his eyes displayed a gentleness that touched her soul.

" For unto you is born this day in the city of David a Saviour, which is Christ the Lord."

The words pounded in Lillie's head. A Savior? Her Savior? Could it be possible that Jesus Christ came to earth as a baby in order to save her soul from eternal damnation?

" And suddenly there was with the angel a multitude of the heavenly host praising God, and saying, Glory to God in the highest, and on earth peace, good will toward men." Garrett's deep voice read on, but Lillie could no longer stand her own discomfort. Without a word, she got up and left the house.

The cold night air cut into Lillie's face. She was glad for

the warmth of her long-sleeved wool dress. Looking up into the black, moonless night, Lillie could count hundreds of stars. She thought of the star that led the wise men to find the baby that would save them from their sins.

"How could it be that You would love me enough to send Your only child to give me eternal life?" Lillie asked toward the sky, not knowing how else to speak to God.

The wind echoed in the pines, but no other answer came to Lillie's questioning heart. "Why can't I remember his face?" Lillie questioned. "Jason's only been dead a year, but when I close my mind it isn't his face I see. It isn't his arms I feel around me. Why is that, God?" Lillie asked earnestly. "And while I'm asking questions, what am I suppose to do about all this?"

The question surprised Lillie, but she suddenly remembered Garrett's words about salvation. He'd told her that she needed to repent of her sins. Well, she certainly felt the need to do that. The hatred and anger she'd carried around hadn't offered her any comfort.

"I may be doing this all wrong, God, but the truth is I'm sorry for the way I've been acting," Lillie began as she hugged her arms to her body. "Garrett told me that You'd forgive me if I asked You to and if I was genuinely sorry, so if that's true, then I guess You just forgave me."

Lillie paused as she tried to remember what else Garrett and the others had shared with her. "I guess the rest is a matter of faith. Maggie said You know everything, so You must know how hard trusting is for me. But the way I look at it," Lillie added, "I don't have any reason not to believe.

If seeing is believing, then watching Jenny and David, as well as Maggie, Garrett, and Daniel, has surely convinced me that there is something worthwhile in putting my trust in You. I want eternal life, God. I want to put the past behind me and know that I have a future home in heaven. So if it's all right with You," Lillie said with tears in her eyes, "I'd like for You to consider me Your child."

The wind picked up until it made a low moaning sound as it filtered through the buildings of the ranch. Lillie lifted her face to the sky and, though the cold was numbing her skin, her heart began to thaw.

"I hope I did the right thing," Lillie murmured.

She jumped at the warmth of the Indian blanket Daniel wrapped around her, pulling her inside its folds with her back against his chest. "You did the right thing," he whispered against her hair.

For several moments, neither Lillie nor Daniel moved. Lillie felt at peace for the first time in her life. Even as a little girl, she'd only felt comfortable when she knew that she could control the outcome of her circumstances. This was different, however, and Lillie readily handed control of her life to the Savior Who'd come as a baby on that Christmas morn so long ago.

Lillie also relished the strong arms that held her so tightly. She leaned back against the well-muscled chest and sighed. Daniel had helped her in so many ways. He'd taken her mind off her selfish pain and put it into a positive direction. Daniel had been a source of healing for Lillie, and she felt the need to thank God for sending him into her life.

"Thank you, God," Lillie whispered, and Daniel presumed she was thanking Him for her salvation.

fourteen

January arrived in unexpected fierceness. Pinon Canyon and the surrounding area usually enjoyed moderate temperatures even in the winter, but not that year. The first blizzard arrived shortly after Christmas, and two more followed close on its heels.

When David managed to get word to Garrett, it was to tell him that the mission had been inundated with new arrivals. Many of the Pueblo people were seeking shelter from the fierce winter weather, and the mission was unable to handle the numbers without additional supplies.

"I hate to leave the ranch with Maggie so near to having the baby, but David said several of the Indian children may have pneumonia," Daniel said as he and Garrett readied a wagon full of supplies.

"The baby isn't due for three weeks by your calculations. I don't think God brought us this far, just to let us down now," Garrett said as he tightened the tarp rope. "I think it's important that we help David and Jenny."

"Aren't you at all worried about leaving Maggie?" Daniel questioned.

Garrett pulled up the collar of his fleece-lined overcoat. "I've put Maggie in God's hands, Daniel. If I take her back now, it'd be like saying that God can't handle the job. He's proven His ability enough for me to trust His promises," Garrett said with confidence. "Besides, Lillie's here and she won't let Maggie get away with anything." Both of the men laughed and went in search of a cup of hot coffee before embarking on the long drive to the mission.

Mack appeared at the kitchen door just as Garrett and Daniel were going inside.

"We're all ready, Garrett," he said with a glance to the western ridge and added, "Looks like a powerful snow to the west. Are you sure you want to try this today?"

"I don't think we have much choice. We're going to tell the ladies goodbye and grab a cup of coffee, and we'll be ready to go," Garrett said as he followed Daniel into the house. "You want to join us?"

"Naw, I've had a gut full of coffee. I'll go wait with the wagons," Mack said and moved out across the yard.

The warmth of the adobe house invited the men to linger, but duty urged them out into the cold.

"I wish you didn't have to go," Maggie finally broke down and said.

Garrett gently brushed his finger along her jawline and then let his hand cup her chin. "I'll be back before you know it, so you just sit here and mind my child."

Maggie moved uncomfortably and allowed Garrett to help her to her feet. "I promise I'll be good," she said with a smile.

"No more cocoa?" Garrett grinned and kissed her on the forehead.

"No more cocoa," Maggie said as she relished the warmth of Garrett's embrace.

Daniel was already at the back door, giving Lillie last minute instructions. "If anything happens, anything at all, you send someone for me right away."

"Don't worry. I remember everything you told me, and I won't waste any time if Maggie needs you," Lillie said as she stood gently fingering the oval locket Daniel had given her for Christmas.

Daniel smiled as he did any time he noticed her wearing it. Lillie looked every bit the prim and proper lady with her starched, high-necked shirtwaist and lavender plaid skirt. The necklace fell in stately grace to hang just below her collar.

Lillie had gifted Daniel with a picture of herself and felt it paled in comparison to his gift. Daniel, however, thought nothing of the kind and kept the picture in his pocket.

"Please be careful," Lillie suddenly whispered.

"Don't worry. We'll be back before you know it," Daniel said.

Lillie had hoped that Daniel would kiss her goodbye, but Garrett appeared in the doorway and they were on their way, leaving Lillie to watch as they rode out of sight.

By noon two inches of new snow covered the ground, with more coming down in huge downy flakes. Lillie occupied herself with baking and cleaning, stopping from time to time to visit with Maggie, who'd spent most of the day in the library.

"How do you feel?" Lillie asked as she looked up from the potato she was peeling to find Maggie in the kitchen doorway.

"I wish I could say wonderful, but that would be a lie," Maggie answered as she poured herself a glass of water and took a seat across from Lillie at the table.

"It won't be much longer," Lillie offered in encouragement. "The time will pass before you know it, and then you'll be so happy enjoying that new baby that you will have forgotten all about the trouble of getting it here."

"I know you're right, but it feels more like a herd inside

me than a baby," Maggie said with a sigh and got to her feet. "I think I'll get this baby a piece of milk toast."

"Maybe you should graze on some corn," Lillie joked and added. "Either way, you stay here, and I'll get some bread from the pantry." Lillie quickly crossed the room to the open pantry door.

Maggie laughed, but her amusement was short-lived. Doubling over, Maggie cried out in pain. "Lillie, I think it's the baby!"

Lillie came rushing back, the color drained from her face as she sized up the situation. Maggie tried to support herself by holding onto the table.

"Maybe you got up too fast," Lillie suggested.

Maggie straightened up and tried to smile. "I don't think so, Lillie."

"I suppose we'll know soon enough," Lillie replied in a worried tone. Daniel and Garrett wouldn't be home for hours, and a gnawing fear was beginning to fill Lillie's mind.

Maggie noticed the deep frown etched on the face of her best friend. "Don't worry, Lillie. Daniel said it would take quite a while for the baby to be born. Send a rider after the men, and we'll be fine."

Lillie's expression softened a bit. "I'm sorry. I didn't mean to worry. Here I am a nervous wreck when you're the one having the baby." Lillie tried to laugh, but the sound remained muffled in her throat.

"I suppose I should go to bed," Maggie said as she moved gingerly across the room.

Lillie was at her side in a heartbeat. "You'd better lean on me in case another pain comes." Maggie nodded and allowed Lillie to help her to her room.

"Where are your nightgowns?" Lillie questioned as she helped Maggie to sit on the edge of her bed.

"In the bottom drawer," Maggie said and pointed toward the large mahogany dresser.

"I'll get one for you, and while you undress, I'll send for the men," Lillie said as she brought Maggie the nightgown. "Will you be all right until I get back?"

"I'll be fine," Maggie said, trying to sound convincing.

Lillie managed to locate a man who assured her that he'd send someone after Daniel and Garrett. On her way back to the house, Lillie grabbed an armful of wood for the fireplace in Maggie's room. There was so much to do, and the thought that Daniel might not make it back in time haunted Lillie throughout her duties.

Despite her fears, Lillie began to gather the things she was certain they would need for the birth of Maggie's baby.

"Lillie! Come quickly!" Maggie called from her bed.

Lillie made her way to the bedroom only to find Maggie sitting on the edge of her bed, drenching wet.

"My water broke," Maggie said, fear thick in her voice. "Lillie, the baby is coming much quicker than Daniel said it would!"

Lillie tried to remain calm. She knew it was important to put Maggie's fears at rest. "Can you make it to your dressing room if I help you?" Lillie questioned. "I'll change the bedding and bring you a dry nightgown."

"I don't know," Maggie grimaced as she tried to stand.

Maggie got to her feet and put her arm around Lillie's neck. Lillie put her arm around Maggie's waist and helped her to a chair.

"Wait here, and I'll bring you something dry," Lillie

said, going back to the dresser to retrieve the promised nightgown. "Are you all right, Maggie?" she called from the bedroom.

"Yes," Maggie answered weakly. Despair filled her heart. Where were Daniel and Garrett? She wanted so badly for them to be at her side that when Lillie came to her with the gown, she made a request.

"Please, Lillie. Pray with me," Maggie begged. "I'm afraid."

Lillie hugged her friend closely. Praying aloud was something she felt quite uncertain about, but Lillie reasoned it would put her own mind at ease as well.

"Of course I will, Maggie. Just remember, I'm not very good at it," Lillie said as she took hold of Maggie's hand. "Dear God, we need help. I'm asking for a miracle that would bring Daniel and Garrett back to the ranch. I'm asking, too, that until they return You'd show me what to do and how to help Maggie. Amen."

Maggie smiled. It was the first time she'd heard Lillie pray. "You did a great job, Lillie. Thank you."

Lillie patted Maggie's hand. "Let me help you change. Then we need to get you back into bed." Maggie nodded and allowed Lillie to slip the wet gown over her head and replace it with a dry one.

With Maggie safely back in bed, Lillie continued her search for the things she thought Daniel might need for the baby's birth. The time away from Maggie gave Lillie a few moments of painful reflection. She remembered the first time she'd felt her own baby move within her. Without thinking, Lillie's hand went to her stomach. How she longed for the baby that had once been there.

Lillie felt the wetness on her cheek before she realized

that she was crying. It was difficult to face the past with any kind of assurance that the future would hold something better. She knew that her life was now different. No, she thought, not just different. Her life had truly improved since she'd accepted Christ as her Savior. But did that mean that life would be less painful? It didn't mean that for Daniel, Lillie thought as she wiped away a tear.

She gathered up several baby blankets that Maggie had lovingly embroidered for her coming child. Lillie felt alone. She gently traced the stitching that outlined a fat puppy and sobbed quietly.

"God, Maggie told me that my baby is in heaven with You. I'm glad he's not alone like me," Lillie said as her tears fell onto the blanket. "But God, if You really care about me, if You really do forgive me for the way I acted toward You, please, please take away this pain." Suddenly, Lillie felt compelled to find a Bible.

Not wanting to upset Maggie with her tears, Lillie went to the library. The family Bible rested on a hand-tatted doily atop a small oak table. She went to the table and reached out, almost fearful of touching the worn pages.

She opened the Bible and gasped as the pages fell to the same place in Luke that had upset her so deeply on the train. Lillie forced herself to look past the ominous warning to the verses below that. When she caught sight of the word *lilies*, she read the words aloud.

"Consider the lilies how they grow: they toil not, they spin not; and yet I say unto you, that Solomon in all his glory was not arrayed like one of these.'" Lillie was not sure of the meaning of the words in Luke twelve, so she read on. " If then God so clothe the grass, which is to day in the field, and to morrow is cast into the oven; how much more will he clothe you, O ye of little faith?"

Hadn't Daniel said faith was the key? Lillie considered the words and the burden of her heart grew lighter. She had to have the faith that God would do the things He had promised. If He was willing to provide for the simple needs of clothing and food, surely God would provide for the deep needs of her pain-filled heart.

Lillie's eyes fell to the thirty-fourth verse and she smiled. "For where your treasure is, there will your heart be also." Her treasure was in heaven not only because her departed loved ones were there, but even more so because her God reigned there. Her God! It felt good to claim God as her own.

Making her way back to Maggie, Lillie had new confidence. God was with her, and nothing else mattered.

Garrett stared in amazement at the parade of people before him. The wagons had been barely three hours away from the ranch when David Monroe had appeared with at least twenty Pueblo men and women behind him.

"What are you doing here?" Garrett questioned as David approached his wagon. Daniel had come from one of the other wagons to echo Garrett's question.

"Yeah, what are you doing out here in the snow with all these people?" Daniel asked as he gave his brother a hearty embrace.

"I woke up at dawn and the Lord put it upon my heart that I needed to gather as many people as possible and meet you on the trail. I don't really know why, but the feeling was so strong I couldn't ignore it," David replied. "We even brought the horses to pack the supplies back to the mission."

"There's really no need for that," Garrett argued. "After all, the wagons are already packed, and we're well on our way."

"No," David insisted. "It may seem illogical to everyone else, but I know that God intends for us to pack these supplies back to the mission by ourselves. Don't ask me why, but I am confident of God's instruction. He always has a purpose for everything He does.

"What about the children you were worried might have pneumonia?" Daniel questioned.

"Fit as fiddles," David said with a shrug. "God works wonders and apparently this time He intends for you to be back at the ranch."

"Well at least take the wagons. I can't see repacking everything onto the horses. You can return the wagons when the snow clears," Garrett suggested.

"That sounds like a wise idea. Why don't we set up a shelter and have some lunch. After that we'd both be wise to be on our way," David said and then turned to instruct several men to erect the tent he'd brought with them.

Half an hour later, the tent was up and the ground inside was swept free of snow. Garrett and Daniel sat with David and the others to enjoy hot coffee and fried ham and tortillas.

"This coffee sure hits the spot," Daniel said as he poured himself another cup. Several Pueblo women entered the tent with still more food, and David motioned them to bring it to where he, Garrett, and Daniel sat.

The sound of a lone rider drew everyone's attention to the opening in the tent. The snow-covered rider rushed into the tent and glanced around, looking for Daniel and Garrett.

Garrett got to his feet, knowing that his ranch hand wouldn't have come so far without a reason. "Joe? Is that you?" he called to the rider.

"It sure is, Boss. I never expected to find you so soon. Figured I'd have to ride all the way to the mission. You and Doc need to get back to the ranch. Miss Maggie's gonna have her baby."

Daniel tensed and David put a hand on his shoulder. Garrett cast a fearful look at David and then Daniel. "But you said the baby wasn't due for weeks. Does this mean something's wrong?"

Daniel wished he could ease Garrett's fear, but reminders of his inadequacy and failings were creating grave concerns in his mind.

"Of course nothing is wrong," David said encouragingly and motioned to one of the Pueblo men. "The doctor is needed at the ranch house. Will you please saddle two horses? You may use my saddle for one of the pack horses, as I'll be driving one of the wagons back to the mission."

"You can use my tack, but my horse is pretty tuckered," Joe offered. "I'll stay on and help get the wagons to the mission, if that's okay with you, Garrett."

"I'd appreciate that, Joe. Come on Daniel, we'd better hurry."

Daniel's face betrayed his concern. Could he be of value to Maggie and Garrett, or would this be like the other times? Would he have to face his best friend with the death of his wife and child, or would God bless his efforts by allowing both Maggie and the baby to be healthy and safe?

David sensed his brother's misgivings. "Daniel, you're going to do just fine. I think it'd be nice if we share a prayer before you go."

"I think that makes a heap more sense than worrying," Garrett agreed and pulled off his black Stetson. Daniel nodded and bowed his head, knowing that his strength came from God. The offered prayer was like crutches to a lame man, bolstering him in spirit and confidence.

When David finished, Garrett lifted his face in a broad grin. Gone were the worry and concern. "God knew where we'd need to be in order to help Maggie and Lillie," Garrett said to Daniel. "He sent David on his way long before we even knew that we needed him." At this David nodded suddenly fitting all the pieces together. Garrett continued, "Since God planned this thing out so far in advance, I'd be an ungrateful fool to worry. Come on Daniel. I want to be there when my child is born."

fifteen

With every contraction, it became more and more apparent that Maggie's labor was progressing faster than Lillie had anticipated. With every pain, Lillie sought ways to ease Maggie's suffering. Ever in the back of Lillie's mind was the possibility that something could be wrong. She prayed fervently that Daniel would arrive and relieve her of the responsibility that demanded life and death decisions.

Lillie wiped Maggie's sweat-soaked brow. "Would you like a sip of water?"

Maggie shook her head. Her hair was spread out across the pillow, hopelessly tangled from her thrashing. She prayed that the ordeal would soon be over, but she feared that it might never end. Exhaustion was quickly overtaking her.

"Lillie," Maggie barely breathed the word. "Has there been any word of Garrett and Daniel?"

"Not yet, but don't worry. I'm sure they'll be here soon. I've prayed about the matter and I have great faith that God will help us," Lillie replied.

Maggie had to smile in spite of the fact that another contraction was overtaking her. "Oh, Lillie, this time is different," Maggie moaned. "I think the baby is coming now!"

Lillie bit her lip and pulled back the covers. She couldn't suppress a gasp. Maggie began to cry out and Lillie did the only thing she could; she prepared to deliver her best friend's baby.

While Lillie prepared blankets for the baby's birth, she prayed repeatedly. "Please God, send Daniel. I need him." She hadn't realized she was praying out loud until a hand fell upon her shoulder.

"I'm here, Lillie." Daniel hadn't even pulled off his snow-covered coat.

"Thank God!" Lillie said, and tears formed in her eyes. Her hands were trembling as she helped Daniel pull off his coat.

"Don't cry, Lillie. Everything is going to be all right," Daniel whispered.

Garrett was already by Maggie's side, soothing her with his words and smoothing back the tangled hair that fell across her face. He tried to remain calm, but the sight of his wife in such agony prompted him to question Daniel.

"Can't we do anything to help her?"

Daniel smiled and finished washing his hands. Lillie handed him a towel and waited for further instructions.

"Maggie's about to have all the help she needs. As soon as this child is born, the pain will go away. As far as I can tell," Daniel said as he examined Maggie, "that's going to be in just a few more minutes."

Lillie worked well with Daniel. Her fears were laid aside as he performed with confident ease. At two minutes before six that evening, Maggie gave birth to her baby.

"It's a girl!" Daniel said as he handed the crying infant to Lillie. "Clean her up, Lillie. Do just like I told you, clear her mouth and get her warmed up."

Lillie's tears fell on the tiny, wrinkled baby. Taking a warm, wet cloth, Lillie gently cleaned the baby's face, laughing at the baby's impressive amount of coppery hair that looked exactly like Maggie's. As Lillie dressed the baby, brilliant blue eyes cried up at her in protest.

"Hush, little one. I'm your Aunt Lillie, and I'm going to get you ready to meet your momma and papa."

"What will you call her?" Daniel asked the proud parents.

"I thought it might be nice if we named her after our mothers," Garrett replied. "Daughtry for Maggie's mother and Ann for mine."

"Daughtry Ann Lucas," Maggie tried the words. "I like it very much."

Lillie brought the baby to Maggie and Garret and placed her in Maggie's arms. "Daughtry Ann, meet your momma and papa," Lillie said with joy in her voice. Her eyes still betrayed her tears, but they were tears of happiness.

"Oh, Garrett, she's beautiful!" Maggie exclaimed.

"She ought to be," Garrett said and planted a kiss on Maggie's forehead. "She looks just like her mother."

Maggie's face was angelic in her joy. She lifted her face to meet Garrett's eyes and never had she loved anyone more. Daughtry began to fuss as if protesting the absence of her mother's attention.

"I image that this little one is hungry," Daniel said as he helped Lillie clean the room. "I think maybe Lillie and I should leave you three alone. Maggie, if you have any trouble at all, send Garrett for me."

"I'm sure we'll be fine," Maggie said as she ran her finger along the velvety cheek of her new daughter.

" I will praise thee; for I am fearfully and wonderfully made: marvelous are thy works; and that my soul knoweth right well," Garrett quoted as he touched the fluffy silk of

Daughtry's hair.

"That's beautiful, Garrett," Lillie said as she started to follow Daniel from the room. "Where is that from?"

"Psalm 139, verse fourteen. The whole chapter is beautiful, Lillie. I think you'd like it."

"Thank you, Garrett. I'll look into it later." With that, Lillie walked down the long west wing of the ranch house. She felt an urgency in her heart to find Daniel.

She nearly ran the rest of the way to the library and then to the sitting room before finally locating him. When she burst through the doorway, Lillie halted, abruptly taking hold of a nearby chair to steady herself.

Daniel looked up from where he stood staring out the window at the snowy night. He smiled a reassuring smile and it was all Lillie needed. She threw herself across the room and into Daniel's waiting arms.

Tears fell in heated intensity against Daniel's shirt. "I didn't think you'd get here in time. I was so scared," Lillie sobbed. "I kept thinking, What if something is wrong, or what if I don't do something right. Oh, Daniel, I prayed and prayed that you'd get here in time."

"Shhh." Daniel held Lillie tightly, surprised at the display of vulnerability. "Hush, Lillie. I'm here now."

"But, Daniel, it could have been so awful," Lillie said as she pulled away from his embrace.

"But it wasn't," Daniel said as he reached out and cupped her tear-streaked face. "God heard our prayers, Lillie. He heard them and answered. Maggie is fine and the baby is fine. You did a good job, Lillie. You'd make a first-rate nurse."

Lillie reached up to wipe away her tears, but Daniel pushed her hand aside. He leaned down and gently began to kiss the tears that dampened her cheeks until his lips found his way to her mouth.

When he pulled his face away from hers, Lillie could see that he was looking at her with new intensity. Could it be more than mere concern, she wondered? Could it be love? Did she want it to be love?

"Lillie, you amaze me," Daniel whispered.

"Why is that?" Lillie questioned.

"You're like a fine china doll. So petite and delicate. You looked so fragile the first time I met you; I was certain that you would break under the misery that followed you."

"I would have never imagined that you cared. After all, I was quite unsightly," Lillie remembered.

"You have never been unsightly, Lillie. If you had been three times that size, you would have still been a beautiful woman," Daniel said honestly. "The weight never worried me as much as the depression."

Lillie pulled away from Daniel and walked across the room. She felt the need to forget the past and distance herself from it, yet there was a need to speak of it.

"I wanted to die," Lillie said. "I thought about throwing myself off of the train."

"I know," Daniel said as he came to stand a few feet away.

Lillie whirled around. "You knew? How?" she questioned.

Daniel remembered the scene as if it had been the day before. "I was on the other side of the door. I saw you standing there, and I knew that you were contemplating your death."

Lillie let the knowledge soak in. "And what would you have done if I'd, if I'd. . . ?" Lillie couldn't seem to form the words.

"I'd have been out the door in a flash and taken you in hand," Daniel whispered. "I would never have allowed you to die. Why do you think I goaded you so much?"

"I presumed because I disgusted you," Lillie answered honestly.

"Never!" Daniel exclaimed. "Nothing could be farther from the truth. I had to give you something to fight for. You'd given up on life, so I had to find the one thing that would affect you strongly enough to fight back."

"My vanity?" Lillie smiled. "How obviously vain I must have appeared."

Daniel grinned. "You were quite the grand lady."

"Well, it worked. I don't think I've ever been angrier in my life," Lillie admitted.

"I know," Daniel said with some regret. "I never wanted you to hate me."

"That's good," Lillie murmured, "because I never did. I hated myself and I hated God, or at least I thought I did, but I've never hated you."

"I'm glad you accepted God's place in your life," Daniel said as he watched Lillie intently. "Then again, I'm glad God helped me to find my way back. I think God's been good to both of us."

"That's true," Lillie agreed. She clasped her hands tightly in her lap. "I never thought I'd come to understand, but today especially, I've never felt closer to God. I feel absolutely glorious," Lillie exclaimed while glancing toward the darkened window. With a smile she turned to Daniel, "I want to feel the snow on my face," she laughed as she went to the door.

The moon tried desperately to peek out from behind the

veil of gray snow clouds. When the moonlight reflected on the snow-covered ground, it sparkled and shimmered like cut crystal. Tiny white flakes were still falling and Lillie raised her arms up in the air as if to receive each one individually.

"You'll catch your death out here," Daniel said as he leaned against the door frame.

"I don't care," Lillie said as she pulled the pins from her hair. "It's glorious and I just want to enjoy the wonder of it all." She whirled round and round in a circle until Daniel's hands fell upon her waist and he began to waltz with her in the snow.

When they finally came to a stop, Daniel was the first to speak. "God was so good to send you to me, Lillie."

Lillie swallowed hard. "Do you really believe that, Daniel?"

"More than ever," Daniel said in a hushed whisper. "God sent you to me, Lillie, and I don't intend to let you get away."

Lillie's eyes grew wide. "And what does that mean?"

Daniel roared a heartfelt laugh. "It means everything, Lillie. Absolutely everything."

Lillie had hoped for a clearer answer, maybe even some declaration of love. Before she could question Daniel further, however, she began to shiver.

"Come on, we're going in," Daniel said as he pulled Lillie back toward the door.

"But I don't want to," Lillie argued. "I want to remember this night forever. The baby and Maggie; Garrett's proud face; and. . . ," Lillie paused, unable to continue.

"And?" Daniel questioned, his laughing eyes still sparkling from the pleasure of having had Lillie in his arms.

Lillie hesitated. Dare she share her heart? What did she know of her heart? There was a time when she thought she understood perfectly well. A time when things seemed much clearer and more easily planned out. But that was then. She cast a sideways glance at Daniel's face and lowered her eyes quickly.

"And?" Daniel pushed her for an answer as he placed his hand on her shoulder.

"And you," Lillie whispered, but it wasn't enough for Daniel. He needed to know more before he could be sure of his own feelings. He reached out and took hold of Lillie's arm, forcing her to turn and face him.

"What about me?"

Lillie felt her breath quicken. "I'm not sure what you mean."

A smile played on Daniel's lips. "I think you know exactly what I mean, Lillie. I want you to admit what you're feeling for me."

Lillie pulled loose and backed up against the door. "What I'm feeling for you?" she whispered. "Isn't that rather presumptuous?"

"I don't think so," Daniel said and leaned forward to kiss Lillie.

"Oh no you don't," Lillie said as she easily ducked his embrace and reached for the door handle.

"All right for now, Lillie," Daniel laughed. "But you

can't ignore it forever, and sooner or later you'll have to be honest with yourself—if not with me."

Lillie opened the door and looked over her shoulder. "Perhaps," she said with a hint of smile, "but not tonight."

sixteen

In the days that followed Daughtry's birth, Lillie tended both Maggie and the baby with loving care. It was more than her desire to attend to their needs; the care she provided seemed to satisfy something in Lillie's heart.

Lillie took her instructions daily from Daniel, who himself was quite wrapped up in the finishing of his office and small hospital in Bandelero. She listened intently as he told her what things she should watch for, paid careful attention as he showed her how to do certain things, and in general enjoyed the companionship of working with him on a daily basis.

In the back of Lillie's mind was the nagging reminder that in a week, maybe less, Daniel would move his things to Bandelero. She didn't like to think of spending her days without his company, but she wasn't certain what she should do about it.

"You're awfully quiet today," Maggie said from where she sat propped up in bed.

Lillie, who was tidying the room, stopped what she was doing and sighed. "I guess I have a great deal on my mind. I'd hoped to keep from burdening you with it."

"But we used to tell each other everything," Maggie said as she patted the side of the bed. "Why not sit down and talk to me?"

"I'd like to, but...," Lillie hesitated. "Maggie things are different now. We aren't the children we were when you

158

left Topeka. A lifetime and then some has passed between us, and I'm not sure that we'll ever have back what we had as young girls."

Maggie smiled. "I know we've changed, but I think for the most part it has been for the better. We've endured a lot, that much is true, but I don't think for one minute that we've lost the ability to remain close. Granted, Garrett is my usual confidant in most things. But there will always be things that are just between you and me. Things that Garrett would never care to intrude upon."

"I feel like an intruder at times," Lillie said as she came to sit beside her friend. "You have Garrett and now Daughtry, and I wouldn't wish it any other way. God knows that I thought my sun rose and set by Jason and the baby we planned." Lillie's voice sounded void of emotion, but Maggie knew that her friend's heart was still tender from the loss. Lillie reached out and took hold of Maggie's hand. "I would never want anything but your happiness. You must know that."

"I do," Maggie said as she placed her free hand on top of Lillie's. "You need to realize though, that you are an important part of that happiness. I don't think I could have made it through these past months without you. Especially with the amount of time Garrett has spent away from the house helping see to Daniel's building project."

At the reminder of Daniel's inevitable departure, Lillie frowned. Maggie took note of Lillie's concern and patted her hand. "You don't have to let him get away."

"I know," Lillie said in a resigned tone. How could she explain to Maggie that it seemed impossible to sort out her feelings for the elusive Dr. Monroe?

Daniel had told her the night Daughtry was born that

sooner or later she'd have to come to terms with how she felt about him. He seemed so sure of himself, yet he wouldn't reveal more than a hint of what he was feeling for her.

A warning flashed across Lillie's mind: Don't get too close. Don't care too much. But it was becoming more certain in Lillie's heart that the warning had come too late.

At the sound of Daughtry's fussing, Lillie went to the cradle and brought the tiny girl to her mother. Maggie's eager arms reached out for her daughter. What a blessing this baby had been! Even Lillie was able to take joy in her arrival.

"I'd better get back to work," Lillie said as she ran her fingers over Daughtry's fluffy hair. She wondered if she would ever have a child to call her own.

Then the day that Lillie had been dreading arrived. Daniel announced at breakfast that he was taking the last of his things and would be permanently in residence in his office in Bandelero. Without thinking, Lillie offered to help him pack up the remaining medical supplies.

Daniel readily accepted her offer and managed a bit of good-natured teasing as he and Lillie made their way to his examining room. "Seems like just yesterday I was stitching up your legs."

"In a rather deceitful manner, I might add," Lillie replied. She'd tried to forget what had passed between them that day, but she knew that things had changed between her and Daniel after that episode.

"It wasn't intended as deceit," Daniel said with a flashing smile. "Cunning, artful, and skillful—but not deceitful. I fell back on an old method that I used with frightened children."

"Oh? Didn't you think I knew well enough to let you take care of the problem?" Lillie questioned knowing that she'd had no intention of allowing Daniel to stitch her wounds.

"Who's kidding whom? You never would have remained still if I hadn't put you to sleep. It was all a matter of needed control," Daniel said good-naturedly. He sensed the teasing in Lillie's voice.

"Yes. You needed to be in control, and I wouldn't allow you."

"You still won't," Daniel said in absolute seriousness. Lillie couldn't bear the intensity of his stare.

"I've truly enjoyed helping you," Lillie said rather shyly as she went back to work. "I think I might go back East and become a nurse."

"Why go away? Everything you need to know, you can learn from me," Daniel replied. Lillie wondered if there were hidden meaning in his words.

"But I need formal training to be a nurse," Lillie protested.

"Out here, no one is going to care. The people are going to be grateful that they have someone to tend to their ailments. That's not to say that I wouldn't be the strictest of taskmasters. I happen to believe in thorough training for anyone in the medical field. But," Daniel said as he paused from packing his instruments, "I have confidence that you would learn quickly. I know how devoted you can be."

Lillie considered his words as she worked. She couldn't shake the fear that gripped her heart. What if Daniel left and she never saw him again? She knew that wasn't what she wanted, and yet what could she do or say to keep him close by?

Garrett came in to help take the crates to the wagon, and Lillie could only stand aside and watch as the two men worked together. She moved around the room that had been Daniel's office for nearly as long as she'd been at the ranch. Every time she'd been in this room, it had been Daniel Monroe, the doctor, who had occupied her attention. Outside of this room, however, it had been Daniel Monroe, the man, who had filled her every thought.

Lillie stood alone, staring at the barren room when Garrett came for the last crate. He took note of the sullen look on Lillie's face and smiled. He couldn't explain to her that he'd just left Daniel with the same look on his face.

"If I didn't know better, I'd think you'd just lost your best friend," Garrett said as he picked up the crate. "But I know that Maggie is doing just fine and is sitting in our bedroom nursing Daughtry at this very minute."

Lillie tried to smile, but the look was short-lived. She turned and acted as though she were double checking the drawers of the desk that Daniel had used.

"Why don't you tell him how you feel?" Garrett finally questioned. He put the crate back on the floor and pushed his Stetson back on his head. "I mean, that is the reason you're moping around here, isn't it?"

Lillie's head snapped up. Garrett's face wasn't mocking or sarcastic, rather it was compassionate, almost pained. Garrett really cared about her in a brotherly fashion, and Lillie was quite fond of his boyish charm and kindness.

"I don't know," Lillie lied and then thought better of it. "No, that's not exactly true," she added.

"I know it isn't," Garrett said softly. "So why not face up to how you feel."

"Because I'm not sure it's real," Lillie blurted out. She

turned away from Garrett and bit her lip. Her hands were twisting the material of her starched, white apron when Garrett turned her to face him.

"Lillie," he said taking her hands in his. "I'm not usually one to give advice and I certainly hate to presume upon feelings, but what have you got to lose? I know you care about Daniel. Why not tell him?"

"I guess because I'm so unsure of myself."

"Then why not pray about it?" Garrett asked.

"I'm pretty new at the Christian life, Garrett. I don't always do things the way you do," Lillie admitted.

"Prayer is the first thing we ought to think to do. I must say, though, I'm not always as good at it as I'd like to be. All I can say is this: God listens and He answers."

"What if the answer is no?" Lillie questioned.

"Well Lillie, that's a chance we all take, but isn't it better that a thing be what the Lord desires?"

Lillie nodded her head. "I suppose you're right. I'm so afraid, though," she said in a voice so childlike that Garrett could almost forget she was nearly twenty years old.

"There is no fear in love; but perfect love casteth out fear," Garrett quoted from 1 John 4.

"But what if it isn't perfect love?" Lillie asked.

Garrett smiled and squeezed Lillie's hands. "Perfect love is God's love, Lillie. That verse tells us that we don't need to fear anything as long as we're a part of God's love. God wants only the very best for His children and therefore we don't need to fear the results. If God's answer is no, it's going to be that way for a very good reason. He's a loving Father, Lillie. Just as I would keep Daughtry from going near a hot stove so she wouldn't get burned, God often tells us no for our protection. It wouldn't be any different if the answer was yes. Trust God, Lillie. Give it over to Him in prayer and trust Him for the answer."

Lillie looked into Garrett's sympathetic eyes and found a good friend in this man her best friend had married. "I'll pray about it, Garrett. But what if God doesn't answer in time?"

"He always answers in time, Lillie. You need to have faith that He will. I would suggest in the meantime that you go tell Daniel goodbye. Maybe it won't be as bad as you think." Lillie nodded, and after Garrett picked up the crate again, she followed him out to the wagon.

"Well, Daniel," Garrett said as he hoisted the crate into the back of the wagon, "this is the last of it." His breath made a steamy cloud in the cold, January air.

Lillie hung back as Daniel embraced Garrett and thanked him for his help. "I could never have gotten this far without you. You've been a blessing and a good friend, Garrett. I'm looking forward to our partnership."

Garrett hugged his friend and patted him heartily on the back. "We're the fortunate ones, Dan." Garrett took a step back and with the slightest nod of his head, indicated Lillie's presence. "I think I'll get back in the house. It's a mite cold out here for me. Besides, I have a family to tend to."

Daniel nodded and asked, "You'll be by in a day or two, won't you?"

Garrett smiled. "You can rest assured that I will be by as often as I can spare the time. I like to know where my money is going. Besides, if I don't spread the good word about you, nobody will want you tending them."

Daniel laughed. "You just do that. Oh, and Garrett," Daniel paused, "tell my favorite new mother to behave herself and take good care of that baby. She'll be in good hands with you and Lillie."

Lillie grimaced at the reference. She didn't want Daniel thinking of her as Maggie's nursemaid. She stepped forward, grateful that she'd thought to put on her woolen coat before following Garrett outside.

"I'll tell, Maggie," Garrett promised and winked at Lillie as he passed her and went into the house.

Daniel leaned back against the wagon and crossed his arms against the warmth of his heavy overcoat. He silently studied Lillie, wanting desperately to tell her what he was feeling, but wondering if it would make a difference.

Lillie moved closer until she stood within a few feet of Daniel. "I wanted to ask you about your offer."

Daniel raised a questioning eyebrow. "What exactly did you have in mind?"

"Would you really consider training me as a nurse?"

"I told you that I would," Daniel replied casually.

Lillie lowered her face. He wasn't making this easy at all. "What would I have to do?" Lillie asked and then quickly added, "to become a nurse."

"I suppose first of all you'd have to spend most of your time with me."

"So I'd need to move to Bandelero?" Lillie questioned.

"It would help," Daniel replied. He watched Lillie for some indication of what she thought of the idea, but with her face lowered, it was impossible to read her expression.

"But Bandelero is barely a town. I mean, there's no hotel or boarding house. It would be difficult to make a move without a place to stay." Lillie lifted her face slowly, almost fearfully. She was afraid to face Daniel's eyes. He seemed so capable of reading her that it made Lillie feel nervous and guarded.

Daniel wanted to reach out and take Lillie in his arms, but his mind kept his heart at bay. There was no sense in trying to force Lillie to make a decision based on feelings. Feelings were great for the moment, but lifetimes couldn't be successfully built on feelings.

"There's plenty of room at my place," Daniel finally said. "What with the extra hospital rooms we have for patients and all. You'd be welcome to stay with me." His look was so intense that Lillie wanted to look away. She couldn't.

"I don't think that'd be appropriate even by western standards," Lillie replied softly.

"I suppose under the circumstances it might be unsuitable, but there is a way to rectify that," Daniel said as he shifted his weight and knocked snow from one boot against the other.

Lillie's sapphire eyes grew wide. "What exactly did you have in mind?" Lillie questioned with trembling lips.

"You could marry me, Lillie," Daniel said in a low whisper.

Lillie felt her legs go weak. She wished desperately that she could steady herself, but there was nothing to take hold of. She looked past Daniel to the snow-covered mountains, trying to calm her nerves. Had he really proposed?

Daniel stepped forward and held Lillie's arms. "Look at me, Lillie," he demanded and Lillie quickly obeyed. "You must know how I feel. I've cared for you for a very long time," he said as he reached up to smooth back a strand of honey blond hair that the wind had blown loose. "I can honestly say I've cared about you from the first moment I laid eyes on you."

"Cared about me?" Lillie questioned. Was that the same as love, she wondered.

"I've never really been good with words, Lillie. I know what I'm feeling though," Daniel said in a determined manner. "I also know what I want out of life, and I know that I want you to be my wife."

Lillie frowned. He still hadn't said that he loved her. Truthfully, Daniel had never once mentioned love. Maybe he couldn't love her. Maybe he'd given all his love to Katie. Lillie tried to reason away her doubts. She'd lost Jason, but she was able to love again or at least she thought she was.

Daniel noted the frown on Lillie's face. His heart tightened in fear. Had he misunderstood her feelings for him? Had he rushed her too soon with thoughts of marriage? He'd been a widower for six years, but for Lillie it'd barely been a year since she'd lost her husband. Maybe she wasn't ready for this. Maybe she'd never be ready to love him the way he loved her.

Daniel dropped his hands and shoved them into his pockets. "I'm sorry, Lillie. I didn't mean to upset you. I just thought maybe you might want the same thing I did. Look, I need to get on over to Bandelero. You think about what I said. Who knows? Maybe you'll change your mind." Daniel stepped up into the wagon. He wanted to kiss her goodbye, but he forced himself to pick up the wagon reins. "You know where to find me."

Lillie looked up in sheer panic. Her brow was furrowed with lines that betrayed her concern, but she couldn't make herself say the words that would stop Daniel from leaving.

The wind picked up, stinging Lillie's cheeks as it hit the tears that fell upon her face.

"Goodbye, Lillie," Daniel said and then with a flick of the reins, headed the wagon down the drive.

Lillie wanted to run after him, to call out to him to stop, but she remained fixed to the spot where she stood. She felt a tight pain in her throat as a quiet sob escaped her mouth. He was leaving her!

As the wagon moved out of sight, Lillie ran through the snow to the corral fence. She hiked up her skirt and climbed up on the first post to better see the departing wagon. For the first time in her life, a prayer came automatically to her lips: "Dear God, please tell me what to do!"

seventeen

The rest of the day, Lillie moved as in a trance. She couldn't make herself focus on the tasks at hand and managed to burn the bread that she'd counted on having with supper. Hastily she put another batch to rise, but she still couldn't take her mind off Daniel and the proposal of marriage he'd offered.

Why wasn't this simple? Even if Daniel didn't love her, he was good to her and he clearly enjoyed being with her. Lillie tried to rationalize away the need for a committed love.

It would be enough to be with someone who acted loving, wouldn't it? Lillie let her mind wander to all the times she'd spent alone with Daniel. She enjoyed talking with him; that was no secret. She thrilled to his knowledge, savored his teaching of medical treatments, and worked well with him at any task. Hadn't she proven to herself that they were compatible?

When Lillie heard Garrett leave the house, she crept down the west corridor to see if Maggie was awake.

Maggie was propped up, reading a book when Lillie peeked her head inside the room. Maggie smiled and motioned Lillie in.

"I've been hoping that you'd come by," Maggie said with genuine affection. "Come tell me everything that happened between you and Daniel."

Lillie's face betrayed the turmoil in her heart. It had

never been possible to hide her concerns from Maggie. "I'm not sure I know where to start."

"Did you tell Daniel how you felt about him?" Maggie questioned as she put the book aside.

"I tried, but no," Lillie said as she wrung her hands. "I couldn't get the words out."

"So what did you say?" Maggie asked softly as she reached out to still Lillie's hands.

"I told him that I wanted to become a nurse. Of course he already knew that from our earlier conversation. He offered to teach me rather than have me go away to school."

"That seems promising, Lillie. You'd have to spend a great deal of time with him in order to be trained," Maggie said excitedly. "That couldn't hurt your chances of opening Daniel's eyes to how important you are to him."

"Do you really think I'm important to him?" Lillie asked innocently. "I know I could be useful, but I want more than that."

"I think you already mean more than that to Daniel Monroe," Maggie said with a smile. "I've seen the way he looks at you, Lillie. I'm not blind to the ways of love."

"Why do you say love? Do you think Daniel loves me?" There, Lillie thought to herself, the question was finally out in the open.

"Do you want him to love you?"

Lillie got up and began to pace. "I've asked myself the same question. I think back to Jason and the baby and I wonder. Do I have it in me to love again? Do I want someone to love me? The only thing I know for sure is that I'm not sure of anything."

Maggie laughed. "Sounds to me like the rantings of a

woman in love. There's nothing like falling in love to cloud a person's judgment."

Lillie stopped and looked at Maggie. "He asked me to marry him, Maggie."

Maggie's face lit up. Her expression was pure joy. "That's wonderful! So what is this all about? He wants to marry you! How can you stand there so calmly asking me if I think he loves you. Isn't it obvious?"

"I don't know. He never said the words. He told me that he cared, but he never said, 'Lillie, I love you.'"

"Words are easy to say. What do his actions tell you?" Maggie questioned seriously.

Lillie thought for a moment before answering. "The second time I laid eyes on Daniel Monroe, he was holding me in his arms while I cried. There I was, sprawled face down in a plowed Kansas field, crying my eyes out and hating everything and everyone around me. He found me, held me, and stayed with me until I was spent. Then he helped me back to the train and stayed with me for a while. I wanted to hate him for not being Jason, but I couldn't." Lillie became quiet as she thought of other times when Daniel's actions had spoken quite loudly.

Maggie waited silently, feeling that Lillie needed to say more. She could see that Lillie was wrestling with herself, so Maggie offered an unspoken prayer for her friend.

"So many times, Daniel has helped me. Even when he was making comments about my weight, it was for my own good. He told me that much."

"What did he say about that?" Maggie asked softly.

"He told me that he knew I'd given up on life, that I wouldn't fight for it. He felt he had to do something to motivate me to live," Lillie answered honestly.

Suddenly her thoughts took her in a different direction and she sat back down beside Maggie. "It's only been a year, Maggie. Just a short, lonely year since Jason died. Am I being disloyal to contemplate remarrying?"

"Only you can answer that. I will say this much. I knew Jason Philips very well. You know he was named for my father, don't you?" Lillie nodded and Maggie continued, "Our families were close when my mother was still alive. Of course I stayed a good friend with Jason long after she was gone, and I feel I knew him fairly well."

"I know you did," Lillie agreed. "Jason always said you were his best friend after me."

"Remember when you were jealous of the times he would come and talk to me about you?" Maggie reminded Lillie.

Lillie smiled. "Sometimes I'd just as soon forget my acts of irrational stupidity."

Maggie laughed. "I'm setting the stage so to speak. Jason wouldn't want you to mourn him. He's in heaven and perfectly content. Life goes on for you, Lillie, and only you can tell what your heart is comfortable with. If you aren't past mourning Jason, then maybe it is best to forget about Daniel for the time being." Lillie nodded somberly. "However," Maggie continued, "I don't think that is the problem."

"You don't?" Lillie questioned, surprised by Maggie's words.

"No, I don't," Maggie stated firmly. "I think you're afraid to love Daniel, and I think you're afraid to accept his love."

Lillie nodded slowly. "I think you're right, but what should I do about it?"

Maggie took hold of Lillie's hand, "God will show you what to do. Just trust Him and have faith that He'll guide you."

Lillie nodded "I know you're right. Thank you, Maggie. I'll always love you. You allowed me to come here to heal my heartache, and through your family, I've learned about God's love for me. You've given me a precious gift, Maggie."

"No, Lillie," Maggie said as she hugged Lillie. "It was God's precious gift." Lillie nodded.

"Do you need anything before I go to my room?"

"Just for you to be happy and whole," Maggie answered.

Lillie spent most of the evening alone in prayer. She wanted to open her mind and heart to whatever direction God had for her.

Lillie contemplated her life since Daniel had become a part of it. She remembered with a smile the day she'd arrive at Pinon Canyon only to find Daniel already in residence. She was quite surprised to realize that a part of her had been happy, actually relieved to find him there. At least she had known something about him, unlike Mack and the other ranch hands. There was some consolation in familiarity.

Her mind drifted over the last few months. So much had happened. Through all of it, Lillie realized that she'd come to depend on Daniel. It wasn't just the physical attraction or her fascination with medicine. It was Lillie's desire to be Daniel's companion.

Lillie drifted into sleep remembering the little things about Daniel that haunted her every waking thought. The way his eyes were lined from laughter, the way his hands were well-manicured and skilled, and the way he looked at her when he was about to kiss her. These were the images that danced in Lillie's head while she dreamed of dancing in the snow with a laughing, life-loving man. A man she was destined to marry.

Lillie woke with a start. It was the middle of the night and she felt ravenous. Realizing that she'd missed supper, Lillie crept quietly to the kitchen. She was suddenly engulfed in memories of Daniel and the night she'd chased him with the frying pan. She couldn't suppress a giggle as she fingered the skillet.

She found some bread. Probably the same that she'd left to rise and forgotten all about. Some homemaker she was turning out to be! Thankful that someone had thought to bake it, Lillie took a slice, as well as the lamp that sat on the stove, and sat down at the kitchen table.

Lillie ate in the shadowy veil of the dimly lit kitchen. She thought of conversations with Garrett, Maggie, and Daniel. Long after she'd finished her bread, Lillie was still focused on one intimate moment with Daniel. It was after they'd waltzed in the snow; the night that Daughtry had been born.

"Sooner or later," Daniel had said, "you'll have to be honest with yourself—if not with me."

Lillie tightly hugged her arms to her body. The vacancy that flooded her heart was filled with only one thought. Daniel!

"I love you, Daniel Monroe," Lillie whispered. The revelation made her smile. She did love Daniel, and something inside her heart told her that he must love her, too.

The howl of wind outside caused the shutters to knock against the adobe house. The sound had always caused

Lillie to shiver, but not that night. She was flooded with the warmth of contentment and happiness. She knew that her heart belonged to someone else.

"Jason," Lillie whispered into the darkness, "I loved you once, and you'll always have a part of my heart that no one else could ever have. But now," Lillie said with a deep restoring breath, "now, I'm ready to let you go." Lillie knew that her heart and soul were once again mended, healed from the pain and suffering of the past.

With a new vitality, she made her way to her bed and went to sleep. In the morning she intended to find Daniel, but for the time being, it was enough to know he was nearby.

The following morning was to be Maggie's first full day out of bed. When Lillie appeared bright and early, dressed in her warmest riding clothes, Maggie laughed.

"Let me guess where you're headed," Maggie said as Lillie took a seat at the same table where she'd bid Jason goodbye the night before; the same table where she'd come to terms with her love for Daniel.

"I'm going to marry Daniel," Lillie said with more joy on her face than Maggie had seen since her arrival to Pinon Canyon.

Maggie smoothed the apron that covered her brown woolen dress. "I knew that you'd come to your senses," she teased. "What took you so long?"

"I guess some of us are more stubborn by nature than others," Lillie said with a laugh.

Just then Garrett walked into the room and noticed Maggie. For a moment his face grew sober and then a smile began to form at the corners of his mouth. "Mrs. Lucas, you are without a doubt more beautiful with each passing day. I am a fortunate man. Now come here and kiss me like a proper wife."

Maggie put her hands on her hips and winked at Lillie. "You were mentioning stubborn natures," she said as she turned her gaze to Garrett. "I happen to be twice as stubborn as you, Lillie. If Mr. Lucas wants his kiss, he'll have to come get it."

Garrett raised a single eyebrow before turning on his heel to leave the room.

"Oh, all right," Maggie said as she rushed toward his retreating back, "I could never beat out Garrett when it came to tenacious behavior."

Lillie laughed as Garrett turned on his heel and pulled Maggie into his arms. "It's good to see that someone can control her," Lillie said as she got to her feet. "I doubt that Dr. Monroe will have as easy a time with me as you've had with Maggie, however."

Garrett rolled his eyes as he remembered the way he'd struggled to get Maggie to accept him as her husband-to-be. "God help Daniel!" was all that he would say before firmly kissing Maggie on the lips.

"Isn't it wonderful, Garrett?" Maggie questioned as she pulled away from his embrace. "Lillie has decided to accept Daniel's marriage proposal."

"I will upon one condition," Lillie said as she pulled on her warm riding gloves.

"And what condition is that?" Garrett questioned.

"I'll only marry Daniel if he truly loves me. I don't want him only to care about me or want me for a nurse. I need him to love me and I need to hear him tell me," Lillie said somberly.

"I don't think that will be a problem," Garrett said with

a smile. "Are you riding into Bandelero right now?"

"Yes," Lillie replied. "I've packed a couple of bags that I can take with me on the horse, that is if you'll lend me one."

"I'll do you one better than that," Garrett said as he released Maggie. "If Maggie doesn't mind, I'll ride with you to Bandelero. Just to make sure you get there safely."

"Of course I don't mind," Maggie said wistfully, "I just wish I could go, too."

"I appreciate the offer, Garrett, but I wish you'd do something else for me, or at least send someone else to do it."

"Name it, Lillie."

"I want someone to ride over and get David. I intend to marry Daniel today, as long as you're right and he does love me," Lillie replied.

Garrett and Maggie both laughed. "After watching those two love-struck ninnies running around this ranch, trying to avoid each other," Maggie stated, "I don't know how anyone could doubt that they love each other."

"I tell you what, Lillie," Garrett said as he went to the stove and poured himself a cup of coffee. "As soon as I down this, I'll ride with you. The turn to go to the mission is about a mile from Bandelero. You can go on into town and make sure you still want to marry that man, and I'll go after David and Jenny. If I know anything about Jenny Monroe, she certainly won't want to miss her brother-in-law's wedding."

"It's a deal," Lillie answered, the excitement in her voice contagious.

Maggie embraced her friend warmly, unashamed of the tears that fell. "I'm so happy for you, Lillie. I know that

God has special plans for you and Daniel."

eighteen

Daniel moved through the stark cleanliness of his new office. The desk he'd ordered, as well as the medical examination table and cabinets for supplies, had arrived days before, and thanks to the extra help Garrett had recruited, they'd been properly installed. Now the room looked the part of being a doctor's office.

For months supplies had arrived on a regular basis, and Daniel took mental inventory as he checked the drawers and cabinets to insure that they held the proper contents.

He moved to the large back room. Here, four small beds lined the walls on either side of a large aisle. It wasn't all that fancy, Daniel knew, but it would serve its intended purpose should someone from town or the neighboring area need an appendix removed or some other surgery.

For the first time since before Maggie's baby had been born, Daniel faced his medical future with confidence and a note of excitement. It was his personal life that was defeating him. He knew that all the offices in the world were meaningless without Lillie.

Making his way to the adjoining four rooms that formed his new house, Daniel wanted to cringe at the emptiness. The rooms were full enough with furniture and the regular household necessities; Garrett and Maggie had seen to this. But it wasn't a home, and Daniel's heart ached for it to be one.

He walked through the large sitting room. This was the

room that adjoined his office. It was designed to make it convenient to hear anyone who might come knocking on his office door during his off hours. Daniel had to smile at that thought. A country doctor usually didn't have too many hours he could call his own. Since word had spread of his arrival, he'd already tended to several minor and one or two not-so-minor ailments.

Nonetheless, Daniel tried to concentrate on the fact that God wasn't done with him. Daniel prayed that God wasn't done with Lillie, either.

Daniel stirred up the dying fire in the sitting room fireplace until the roaring blaze took the damp chill from the room. He admired the pillows that Maggie had embroidered for his sofa and smiled at the curtains that he knew Maggie and Lillie had worked on together.

Moving from the room, Daniel passed into the smaller sitting room. This one was designed for privacy. A large wood stove had been used in place of another fireplace. Daniel hadn't bothered to spend much time in this more intimate room. He'd agreed to have it made a part of the house when he'd thought that Lillie might consent to marry him. He tried to remind himself that there was still hope, but his heart wasn't convinced.

Off from the sitting room was a small hallway in which Daniel could either turn left and go into the kitchen and dining area, or right and go into the bedroom. He'd spent the night in the huge, four-poster bed that Garrett had given him. Of course, many of the things in the house were gifts from someone. Most of them seemed to come through Garrett, however, and Daniel couldn't have been more grateful for God sending him such a friend and business partner.

If God would only send him a more intimate partner. If only God would answer his prayer and send him Lillie!

Refusing to be defeated by the situation, Daniel started praying: "God, you know how much I need her. You know how much I love her. I felt certain that You were directing me to her and that You wanted me to marry her. If that's the truth, if that's really what I understood, then Lord, please open Lillie's heart to love me, too."

The knock at the office door sounded through the empty house and startled Daniel from his prayer. "No doubt a sore throat or fever to ease my miseries," Daniel said and laughed to himself.

He finished tucking in the tail of his white cambric shirt as he made his way back through the house and opened the office door. He froze in place as his eyes met the sapphire blue of Lillie's quizzical stare.

She stood before him, silent. Suddenly Daniel noticed the bag in her hand. He reached out and took it from her and set it inside the office.

"There's another one on the horse," Lillie said matter-of-factly as she walked past him into the office.

She was taking off her bonnet when Daniel finally found his voice. "I must say, I'm surprised to see you. What have you brought me? Goodies from the kitchen? Surely not more bandages!" Daniel was trying desperately to keep the atmosphere tolerable.

"No. No bandages," Lillie said as she placed her bonnet on the desk and proceeded to remove her coat.

"Then what?" Daniel questioned.

"Clothes," Lillie said simply. She smoothed the wrinkled shirtwaist that she'd worn and reached up to pull her hair free from the pins that had held it within her bonnet's bounds. By this action, Lillie was making a clear statement that she'd come home.

"Clothes?" Daniel questioned, almost afraid to go further. "For me?"

"Not exactly," Lillie whispered. "They're mine."

"I see," Daniel said and slowly closed the office door. "And just what are your intentions, Lillie."

Lillie leaned back against his desk and smiled. This time she wouldn't make it easy on him. Hadn't he tortured her enough times? "My intentions are to become a nurse," Lillie answered. "You told me you could teach me everything that I would need to know."

"I must say, I didn't expect you to have an answer so quickly," Daniel stated in a serious manner. "Have you forgotten the price of my training?"

Lillie smiled coyly. "I haven't forgotten a single thing you said to me, Dr. Daniel Monroe. I'm ready to pay the price."

Daniel stared in disbelief. It was what he'd prayed for, so why should it surprise him?

"You're ready to say yes?" Daniel questioned as he moved toward Lillie. He stopped short of taking hold of her and fought to keep his mind clear so that he could concentrate on her answer.

"That depends on the question," Lillie whispered. She matched his bold stare and reached up to trace the outline of his stubble-covered chin. She could feel him tremble as he took hold of her hand to still its movement.

"Don't toy with me, Lillie. This is serious business."

Lillie laughed. "I think you'll see how serious I am when your brother gets here. That is if you still want to get married. I do seem to remember being asked to marry you.

Is the offer still good?" Lillie questioned in a businesslike manner, trying her best not to give way to her desire to embrace Daniel with all her strength.

Daniel seemed to catch on to her game. He took hold of both of her hands and pulled them to his lips. "I don't need another business partner. I have Garrett for that. What I do need is a wife. But more importantly, I need you, Lillie."

Lillie sighed and moved closer to Daniel. He still hadn't told her that he loved her, and Lillie knew that she needed to know how he felt. She'd still marry him, confident that he would grow to love her, but it was important to know where she stood with him. How could she get him to tell her without coming right out and asking?

As if on cue, Daniel began to speak. "I have to say something, and I want some honest answers from you in return. Will you do that much for me?"

Lillie lifted her face to meet Daniel's. "Of course." Her words were soft and sweet.

"Come with me," Daniel said as he led Lillie to the sofa in the large sitting room. The fire still blazed on the grate and Lillie couldn't resist warming her hands before joining Daniel on the sofa.

"Lillie," Daniel began, almost afraid to speak the words. "I don't want you to rush into this. I can wait for you if I have to. I don't want you to feel forced into a relationship you don't want, just because of what I said to you in the past. I would still find a way to train you as a nurse if that was what you wanted." He paused and a certain sadness was evident in his voice. "Even if you didn't want to marry me."

Lillie nodded. "Go on," she encouraged.

"I've been a widower for six years, but you've only been

a widow for just over a year. We haven't known each other all that long either, and I don't want you thinking you have to marry me out of obligation."

"Obligation?" Lillie questioned. Nothing could be farther from her mind, but she let Daniel continue.

"I think it would be easy to take advantage of your vulnerability, Lillie. I don't want to do that. I don't want you that way, because. . . ." Daniel grew uncomfortable and fell silent.

"Because?" Lillie prodded.

"Because I love you, Lillie!"

Lillie wanted to shout and sing, but instead she tried to remain calm. She steadied her nerves and held her voice in check as she replied, "I see."

Daniel had hoped for more of a response. Surely she'd come to feel the same way in time. Was it wrong to expect that of her so soon after the death of her husband and child?

"I do love you, Lillie. I have for a very long time. Ever since losing Katie, I became a hard man. I didn't want to feel anything inside, that's why I pushed God away. God makes a person take inventory of what's inside his soul and I didn't want to have to deal with that. But then," Daniel paused with a smile. "He got to me in the only area I was vulnerable. He sent you. Lillie, I don't know what you're feeling right now, but since you're here, I know you must feel something. I pray that in time you'll come to love me as much as I love you." Daniel's tone was pleading, but still Lillie refused to give in.

"I'm afraid that's quite impossible," Lillie said with her face lowered to keep from smiling.

Daniel felt his heart breaking. Why was she willing to marry him if she could never love him? Surely she had to know what that would do to a man. Daniel jumped up from the sofa as if it had suddenly become hot iron.

"Impossible?" he questioned and Lillie could no longer bear his misery.

"Yes," she said as she came to him. "It would be impossible to come to love you, because I already do love you, Daniel Monroe. I love you with all my heart."

Daniel's fears fell away and a smile replaced the worried, heartbroken look on his face. "Are you sure, Lillie?"

"Sure enough to spend the rest of my life loving you. Sure enough to work beside you and to have your children," Lillie said confidently. "And Daniel, I do want to have children. Please say you want them, too!"

Daniel crushed Lillie to him and held her so tightly she thought she might snap in two. "I'd love to have a dozen children with you, Lillie. You'll make a wonderful mother and an even better wife. I knew God had sent you for a reason."

"Oh, He had a special reason, all right," Lillie said as she looked up into the eyes of the man she'd soon marry. "He sent me to a place to heal from my hurt and suffering, and then He sent me His love and forgiveness so that I might enjoy eternity in heaven. But He didn't leave me simply hoping and waiting for the end of time. He sent you. He sent you to heal me and to love me, and for that, I am most grateful."

"I love you, Lillie," Daniel said as he lowered his lips to kiss her.

Lillie melted against him and felt her heartbeat quicken as it always did whenever Daniel kissed her. How good God was to see her need when she couldn't see it for herself. How like God to bless her in spite of her denying Him.

"Thank you, Father," Lillie prayed as Daniel held her close. She thought of the future with Daniel and smiled without fear at the thought of it. Perfect love casts out fear, Lillie remembered. God had taken her fear and replaced it with love. Perfect love.

A Letter To Our Readers

Dear Reader:

In order that we might better contribute to your reading enjoyment, we would appreciate your taking a few minutes to respond to the following questions. When completed, please return to the following:

Karen Carroll, Editor
Heartsong Presents
P.O. Box 719
Uhrichsville, Ohio 44683

1. Did you enjoy reading *Perfect Love*?
   ☐ Very much. I would like to see more books
      by this author!
   ☐ Moderately
      I would have enjoyed it more if _____

   _____

2. Are you a member of *Heartsong Presents*? Yes   No
   If no, where did you purchase this book? _____

   _____

3. What influenced your decision to purchase
   this book? (Circle those that apply.)

   Cover   Back cover copy

   Title   Friends

   Publicity   Other _____

4. On a scale from 1 (poor) to 10 (superior), please rate the following elements.

    ___Heroine   ___Plot

    ___Hero   ___Inspirational theme

    ___Setting   ___Secondary characters

5. What settings would you like to see covered in *Heartsong Presents* books?

_____

_____

6. What are some inspirational themes you would like to see treated in future books?_____

_____

_____

7. Would you be interested in reading other *Heartsong Presents* titles?   Yes   No

8. Please circle your age range:

Under 18	18-24	25-34
35-45	46-55	Over 55

9. How many hours per week do you read? _____

Name _____

Occupation _____

Address _____

City _____ State _____ Zip _____

HEARTS♥NG PRESENTS books are inspirational romances in contemporary and historical settings, designed to give you an enjoyable, spirit-lifting reading experience.

AVAILABLE NOW AT A SALE PRICE OF $2.95 each!

- ____ HP 1 A TORCH FOR TRINITY, *Colleen L. Reece*
- ____ HP 2 WILDFLOWER HARVEST, *Colleen L. Reece*
- ____ HP 3 RESTORE THE JOY, *Sara Mitchell*
- ____ HP 4 REFLECTIONS OF THE HEART, *Sally Laity*
- ____ HP 5 THIS TREMBLING CUP, *Marlene Chase*
- ____ HP 6 THE OTHER SIDE OF SILENCE, *Marlene Chase*
- ____ HP 7 CANDLESHINE, *Colleen L. Reece*
- ____ HP 8 DESERT ROSE, *Colleen L. Reece*
- ____ HP 9 HEARTSTRINGS, *Irene B. Brand*
- ____ HP10 SONG OF LAUGHTER, *Lauraine Snelling*
- ____ HP11 RIVER OF FIRE, *Jacquelyn Cook*
- ____ HP12 COTTONWOOD DREAMS, *Norene Morris*
- ____ HP13 PASSAGE OF THE HEART, *Kjersti Hoff Baez*
- ____ HP14 A MATTER OF CHOICE, *Susannah Hayden*
- ____ HP15 WHISPERS ON THE WIND, *Maryn Langer*
- ____ HP16 SILENCE IN THE SAGE, *Colleen L. Reece*
- ____ HP17 LLAMA LADY, *VeraLee Wiggins*
- ____ HP18 ESCORT HOMEWARD, *Eileen M. Berger*
- ____ HP19 A PLACE TO BELONG, *Janelle Jamison*
- ____ HP20 SHORES OF PROMISE, *Kate Blackwell*
- ____ HP21 GENTLE PERSUASION, *Veda Boyd Jones*
- ____ HP22 INDY GIRL, *Brenda Bancroft*
- ____ HP23 GONE WEST, *Kathleen Karr*
- ____ HP24 WHISPERS IN THE WILDERNESS, *Colleen L. Reece*
- ____ HP25 REBAR, *Mary Carpenter Reid*
- ____ HP26 MOUNTAIN HOUSE, *Mary Louise Colln*
- ____ HP27 BEYOND THE SEARCHING RIVER, *Jacquelyn Cook*
- ____ HP28 DAKOTA DAWN, *Lauraine Snelling*
- ____ HP29 FROM THE HEART, *Sara Mitchell*
- ____ HP30 A LOVE MEANT TO BE, *Brenda Bancroft*
- ____ HP31 DREAM SPINNER, *Sally Laity*
- ____ HP32 THE PROMISED LAND, *Kathleen Karr*
- ____ HP33 SWEET SHELTER, *VeraLee Wiggins*
- ____ HP34 UNDER A TEXAS SKY, *Veda Boyd Jones*
- ____ HP35 WHEN COMES THE DAWN, *Brenda Bancroft*
- ____ HP36 THE SURE PROMISE, *JoAnn A. Grote*
- ____ HP37 DRUMS OF SHELOMOH, *Yvonne Lehman*
- ____ HP38 A PLACE TO CALL HOME, *Eileen M. Berger*
- ____ HP39 RAINBOW HARVEST, *Norene Morris*
- ____ HP40 PERFECT LOVE, *Janelle Jamison*

ABOVE TITLES ARE REGULARLY PRICED AT $4.95! USE THE ORDER FORM BELOW AND YOU PAY ONLY $2.95 per book

SEND TO: Heartsong Presents Reader's Service
P.O. Box 719, Uhrichsville, Ohio 44683

Please send me the items checked above. I am enclosing $_____ (please add $1.00 to cover postage per order). Send check or money order, no cash or C.O.D.s, please.

To place a credit card order, call 1-800-847-8270.

NAME_____

ADDRESS_____

CITY/STATE_____ ZIP_____

HPS JULY

add a little MYSTERY to your romance!

TWO GREAT INSPIRATIONAL ROMANCES
WITH JUST A TOUCH OF MYSTERY
BY MARLENE J. CHASE

_____*The Other Side of Silence*—Anna Durham finds a purpose for living in the eyes of a needy child and a reason to love in the eyes of a lonely physician...but first the silence of secrets must be broken. HP6 BHSB-07 $2.95.

_____*This Trembling Cup*—A respite on a plush Wisconsin resort may just be the thing for Angie Carlson's burn-out—or just the beginning of a devious plot unraveling and the promise of love. HP5 BHSB-05 $2.95.

Inspirational Romance at its Best from one of America's Favorite Authors!

FOUR HISTORICAL ROMANCES
BY COLLEEN L. REECE

___ *A Torch for Trinity*—When Trinity Mason sacrifices her teaching ambitions for a one-room school, her life—and Will Thatcher's—will never be the same. HP1 BHSB-01 $2.95

__*Candleshine*-A sequel to *A Torch for Trinity*—With the onslaught of World War II, Candleshine Thatcher dedicates her life to nursing, and then her heart to a brave Marine lieutenant. HP7 BHSB-06 $2.95

__*Wildflower Harvest*—Ivy Ann and Laurel were often mistaken for each other...was it too late to tell one man the truth? HP2 BHSB-02 $2.95

____ *Desert Rose*-A sequel to *Wildflower Harvest*—When Rose Birchfield falls in love with one of Michael's letters, and then with a cowboy named Mike, no one is more confused than Rose herself. HP8 BHSB-08 $2.95

LOVE A GREAT LOVE STORY?

Introducing Heartsong Presents —
Your Inspirational Book Club

Heartsong Presents Christian romance reader's service will provide you with four never before published romance titles every month! In fact, your books will be mailed to you at the same time advance copies are sent to book reviewers. You'll preview each of these new and unabridged books before they are released to the general public.

These books are filled with the kind of stories you have been longing for—stories of courtship, chivalry, honor, and virtue. Strong characters and riveting plot lines will make you want to read on and on. Romance is not dead, and each of these romantic tales will remind you that Christian faith is still the vital ingredient in an intimate relationship filled with true love and honest devotion.

Sign up today to receive your first set. Send no money now. We'll bill you only $9.97 post-paid with your shipment. Then every month you'll automatically receive the latest four "hot off the press" titles for the same low post-paid price of $9.97. That's a savings of 50% off the $4.95 cover price. When you consider the exaggerated shipping charges of other book clubs, your savings are even greater!

THERE IS NO RISK—you may cancel at any time without obligation. And if you aren't completely satisfied with any selection, return it for an immediate refund.

TO JOIN, just complete the coupon below, mail it today, and get ready for hours of wholesome entertainment.

Now you can curl up, relax, and enjoy some great reading full of the warmhearted spirit of romance.